SECOND

SEAT

Book Two of The First Plane Trilogy

PATTI LARSEN

Find out more about Patti Larsen at **pattilarsen.com**

chapter one

The droning sound of my grandfather's voice was the last thing I wanted to listen to this morning. I'd been hearing far too much from him in the past week, something I was quick to realize wasn't about to end any time soon.

Lies, all of it. You know this, Meira. My demon grandmother groused in my head, her spirit thrashing in fury as Henemordonin, Second Seat of Demonicon, expounded to the court how sunny and shiny and full of butterflies and sparkles our plane was. Despite the fact my forces were still at large, patrolling the cities and settlements searching for the Planeless, a cult preaching peace and light to all demons, my grandfather assured the gathered royal family everything was hunky dory.

They don't care, I sent to Ahbi as Henemordonin went on, blocking out his speech, more of the same from

1

yesterday and the day before that and the day before that. *All they want is for things to work in their favor. And if that requires sticking their heads in the sand, they'll do it and be happy for it.*

If only there were something I could do. I'd made illegal the meetings of the cult, set my finest scientist on the task of finding an antidote for the nectar the Planeless used to sway the hearts and minds of the demons they recruited, and ordered the leader of the sect, Xeoniteridone, arrested. All without a scrap of support from my Second Seat.

We already know he's up to something, Ahbi sent as Henemordonin's voice dropped. I'd begun to notice, now I paid attention to his tactics instead of his bullying, the rhythm to his delivery. He always began his presentations with a dire forecast, spinning out the negatives should anyone within hearing range go against him, then led them into his way of thinking. He moved on, offering a dire warning if they failed and finally wrapped up with a positive message to reinforce the notion they needed to trust him and only him.

He learned that from me, Ahbi sent. *Though I gave up using it centuries ago. Got boring.*

I almost laughed. Except our present situation was far from funny. Bad enough my father and former Ruler, Haralthazar, started his demonocracy campaign before I took the throne. But his lack of follow-through left me hanging, scrambling to regain the power he gave away. I spent four years suffering the effects of his decisions, four years under my grandfather's thumb. Four years in which my power was removed further and further from me.

Standing up to him helped. Ahbi shifted restlessly inside me as we both felt the family sway once again to Henemordonin's side. I didn't bother considering a rebuttal. It never did me a scrap of good to fight with him publicly.

Not exactly true, Ahbi sent. *You certainly put him in his place when we confronted the Planeless.* She had it right, and I couldn't have been happier to show my grandfather he couldn't just set me aside and pat my head like a nice little demon. I might have only been eighteen, but I sat in Ruler's seat, not him. And when the Planeless openly and brazenly recruited a massive number of demons from under my nose, I had to act. It still made me anxiously curious why Henemordonin stood against my choice to bring in the army, though I couldn't believe he had anything to do with the cult.

I have to agree, Ahbi sent. *He's too in love with his own power to side with a sect that suppressed the magic of demons. He'd never allow his own to be subjugated.*

We still have no idea what Xeoniteridone's ultimate plan is, I sent. *And where his sorcery came from.* That was a massive shock, discovering a demon with the power of sorcery. According to everyone I knew, it was simply impossible.

Demons didn't have the dark, devouring energy. We were fed by the element of fire instead.

We'll find out, Ahbi sent. *Just as soon as we do something permanent to your grandfather.*

I still shuddered from the idea of having him removed so blatantly. *I know it would make things easier if he were to have an accident*, I sent. *But if we make the attempt and it fails, you know it's going to come back on us.*

It won't fail, she growled. *Sic Mabel on him.*

I did grin this time, squashing my expression quickly. Lucky enough, no one was looking at me and so they missed my amusement. *I only wish*, I sent, thinking of the drach female I'd just started to get to know. *She's gone back with the rest of her people, remember?* Mabel had a distinct dislike for my grandfather and already offered to eat him despite her revulsion at the idea. I would have settled for charbroiled.

We could call her back, Ahbi sent. *I'm sure she'd do it as a favor to you. She likes you.*

I like her, too, I sent. *But the drach are too busy.* The second surprise came, not only for me but for my sister, Syd, who risked everything to save our Universe, including the people she loved. I wished she were here right now, even as I straightened on my throne and reminded myself I was Ruler and didn't need my crazy talented sister to rescue me. Besides, she was off with Max, the leader of the drach, and the rest of the first race, trying to heal the damage Syd's son, Gabriel, did to the veil when he was forced to open a gateway to the other Universe.

I perked as Henemordonin's voice climbed the register, out of the doldrums and into a more normal, brighter tone. "And I can assure you, with the utmost confidence," he smiled, and I swear I caught a sparkle in his eye as he gestured with grand arrogance, "our people, our planes, are safe and secure under my rule."

Oh, he so did not just say that out loud, Ahbi snarled.

I sighed in my head, holding very still as he turned slowly and with absolute deliberation, toward me, still smiling.

"Very well," I said in as bored a tone as I could wrangle while my grandmother raged in my head. "Thank you for your little update, Henemordonin. Was there anything else?"

His jaw jumped. It was oh-so-very hard not to grin in his face. While I had become fearful of him yelling at me, enduring so much abuse I retreated from it, I'd come to find my strength again. In doing so, I took great pleasure in undercutting him in the subtlest ways. I could see why Ahbi loved being Ruler so much in these moments.

My grandfather didn't comment as all the work he'd put into his speech unraveled in a tittering wave of amusement from the court.

Ahbi's anger stilled. *Sizzle*, she sent.

Not done, I sent. "I do hope not," I said, looking away from him with a slow eye roll. "We have more important matters to deal with than yet another long-winded explanation why you are the center of the Universe."

Meira! Ahbi gasped a laugh.

You approve? I gestured to the front of the line where the demons waiting for audience stood. As the first stepped forward, Henemordonin sank into his throne, still glaring at me.

Very well done, she sent, chuckling with evil intent. *Let him chew on that slap in the face for the next few hours.*

I'm less worried about his posturing in court, I sent as I half-listened to the whining of yet another demon noble who wanted something someone else already owned, *and more about Jabuticabron's silence.*

Ahbi's laughter fell quiet. *Agreed*, she sent. *I know Henemordonin is blocking us.*

As long as that's all it is, I sent. *And not that Jabuticabron has been influenced by the Planeless.*

She didn't comment as I listened to Henemordonin pronounce his decision for the demon before me. I'd taken to allowing him to run the minutia of court, though I was careful to handle the big stuff myself. Let him ponder the significance of adultery, theft and scandal. I had more important issues to deal with.

Such as the virulent plague of the cult. We'd already lost many demons to it, the combination of the nectar and Xeoniteridone's coercive power tied to his sorcery making short work of even the most loyal demons. Among them was Rameranselot, a friend and, I hoped one day, my mate.

You're getting ahead of yourself, Ahbi sent. *He's said no in the past.*

The truth of Ram's rejection stung far more than anything Henemordonin could throw at me these days.

He'll come around, I sent. *If we can rescue him and reverse the effects of the nectar.*

He'd gone from faithful guardian/conspirator/friend to rabid follower of the Planeless in a heartbeat, at least according to my guard captain, Jabuticabron. It still amazed me how quickly the change happened and, if I hadn't watched it with my own eyes that night in Bilhaeder, I still wouldn't believe it was possible for ordinary, power-loving demons to willingly give up their magic and their passion for gathering more in exchange for peace and powerlessness.

It makes no sense, Ahbi agreed. *But it's fact.*

I reached for Jabuticabron as Henemordonin continued his Second Seat duties, dealing with the complainants before us. Almost immediately, I felt the wall around him, familiar magic blocking me from reaching him.

Just push through, Ahbi growled. *Your grandfather has earned no respect. Don't even think about taking it easy on him.*

I'd rather he didn't know I was talking with Jabuticabron, I sent. *If Henemordonin wants to hide what's happening from me, there's a good reason for it. I'll get to the bottom of it, even if I have to go through Sequoia.* My guard captain's sister, Avenesequoia, was among my cherished friends and allies. The siblings of my darling silver Persian/demon boy, Sassafras, they had both taken it upon themselves after my arrival on Demonicon to watch over and take care of me. I was grateful for both of them, partly because having them with me felt like Sass was at my side.

I've hardly vanished, his crisp voice broke through.

Eavesdropper, I sent. *Can you reach your brother?*

Not yet, Sass sent. *But Sequoia is on it.*

As long as you allow your grandfather to use the new laws against you, Ahbi sent, cutting Sassafras off, *he will continue to chip away at your influence until no amount of embarrassing him in front of the court will do you a bit of good. You're on your way to being a figurehead, Meira. Don't think he's not working on new laws to bring you down.*

Ruler. Sequoia's mind touched mine, hers flavored with mint and bright yellow light.

I shifted slightly in my seat as she spoke. *What is it?*

Jabuticabron is here, she sent. *But I can't reach him.* I could feel her moving rapidly, her mind anxious. *I caught sight of him being herded by his own guards into your grandfather's office.*

The bastard. Ahbi seized control and tried to force me to my feet. I could only thank the elements for Sassafras who shoved against her so hard, his power joining mine. A soft grunt of expelled air left my lips as we pinned Ahbi together.

I really worry about you, Sass sent to her directly. *You used to be so in control, Ahbi Sanghamitra. What's become of your soul?*

I've been murdered, she snarled, *forced to live inside the Node of Demonicon and not one, but two, Hayle witches.* She almost panted her frustration. *All while the power of my position is being stripped away by a demon I should have had killed on our wedding night.*

Grandmother. I sent soothing energy as she settled, still fuming. *I'm so sorry.* There was a time when we butted heads over her need to control everything. But I'd come to feel terrible for her, empathetic she'd lost everything in her need to protect Demonicon. *It's going to be all right.*

She grumbled and turned her back on me internally, falling silent, her sullen quiet making me sigh again.

Ruler. Sequoia felt stationary now. *Did you want me to try to see Jabut?*

No. I sat up straighter on my throne. *Just keep an eye on him if you can. We'll be done here soon and then I'll come retrieve him personally.*

Sassafras showed me an image of himself, perched on the window seat of my quarters, his amber eyes glowing while he hopped down and sashayed his furry butt to the door.

I'm coming to meet you, he sent to Sequoia. *Meira, I'll see you there.*

Anticipation rose like a ball of fire in my stomach. Henemordonin may have cornered me, cancelled out my ability to confront him directly and done his best to remove what power I had over my people, but I'd be damned if he'd turn me into some figurehead.

chapter two

The moment court wrapped, Henemordonin ran off faster than I could follow. It didn't help, as he left, he informed the entire family I had an important announcement.

"Ruler," he said, stepping down from the throne, "you may proceed." He then retreated while I gaped at him with my mouth open.

He knows you're aware of Jabut's arrival, Sassafras sent. *Get moving, Meira.*

It only took a moment to firmly state I did not, in fact, have anything further to say, but it was long enough for my grandfather to stride off and disappear down the elevator. I pursued him as quickly as I could without looking like I was chasing him. I'm sure everyone knew something was up, because the whispering of the mass of demons I'd begun to see as a single, faceless entity wrapped in fancy clothing and immense hairstyles started long before I was out of earshot.

Henemordonin has just entered his office, Sequoia sent as I impatiently waited for the elevator platform to return to the top of the Seat. *The door is flanked by almost a dozen guards. A new face is giving orders.* She sounded perplexed and very worried. *I do not know this demon.*

I pushed the elevator hard the moment I stepped on board, feeling it drop with such speed I lost gravity for an instant. My platform boots rang on the shining black stone floor, the towering soles propelling me forward as I glared my fury at the large group of demon guards standing outside my grandfather's office.

You failed to bring your own protection, Sassafras sent. *Be careful.*

The Guards were supposed to be loyal to me, but I'd learned long ago, aside from Jabuticabron and a few of his closest friends, the faithfulness of the Guards was as fluid as the Demoniconian power structure.

I was about to find out if they were willing to defy me outright.

Immediately upon my approach, a massively shouldered demon with a thick, black eye patch and half a horn missing on the right side stepped out into the middle of the two flanking rows of guards. His armor seemed coated in some kind of metal instead of the standard dull black. A long, thin mustache hung almost to his chest in curling spirals. His arms and what was exposed of his chest crisscrossed with paler pink scars. Whoever this demon was, he'd seen enough battles I knew simple intimidation would get me nowhere.

"Ruler." He didn't bow, his gravel voice half cough, half snarl.

"Stand aside." I allowed the power of Demonicon to flow around me, Stage One.

"We can't do that," he said in the exact same tone of voice, arms crossing over his chest.

"You will stand aside," I said, the air now crackling with my power as I went for Stage Two, "or I will see you stripped and left empty."

He didn't move a muscle. "The law prevents you from doing so," he said.

I hate him already, Ahbi hissed.

"How dare you defy your Ruler?" I knew I stood in a precarious situation without backup and no real Stage Three, unless I intended to attack my own guards. But I had a feeling, even if I'd brought a full army of demons loyal to me to this particular argument, I would still lose. This demon had the toughened look of a soldier who never backed down from a fight, with Ruler or otherwise.

Do you know him, Grandmother? I couldn't just walk away.

I don't, she sent. *Henemordonin must have brought him up from the ranks.*

"I am obeying the law," he said.

"Your name and plane ranking," I snapped.

"Rutorith," he said. "One hundred and thirteenth plane."

I was right, Ahbi sent. *Too low in stature to be a threat, but high enough to be an officer of some reknown.*

"Your new guard captain," he finished.

"According to whom?" He might as well have slapped me across the face, I was so shocked by his words. Jabuticabron was my guard captain.

"Second Seat," Rutorith said.

"He doesn't have the authority to grant you such a position," I snarled. "Now step aside." This time I pushed with some power, and, to his credit, I felt Rutorith hold his ground.

"He does," the infuriating demon said in the same growly, gravel voice. He still had, as yet, to move a muscle since planting himself in my path. "According to law."

Since when? Ahbi fumed. *This is insanity.*

"I would speak to Second Seat," I said, hands clenching at my sides. "Now."

"He asked not to be disturbed," Rutorith said. "By anyone."

By me, in other words.

Just squash this insect and let's move on, Ahbi sent.

Grandmother. I held my ground. *What is this new law that gives Henemordonin the right to replace Jabut?*

14

I don't know, she sent, tone softening into worry.

Neither do I, I sent. *Which makes me more nervous than eager to charge in there. For all I know, Henemordonin is waiting for me to do so as a means to take me down.* A shiver of nerves woke and danced in my belly. What other laws might have been snuck past me? But how could he have done so without me knowing? I'd been so careful lately.

We need more information, Sassafras interrupted suddenly. *I know it sucks, but you have to back off, Meira.*

You're kidding, right, Sass? There was no humor in my answer.

He sighed. *I'm sorry, but you know I'm right.*

I stared in Rutorith's one deep amber eye and relented.

"Tell Henemordonin I wish to speak to him the moment he's free." I retreated, fury boiling, frustration and contempt both for my grandfather and my own lack of action making me tremble.

Rutorith finally moved from his statue-like stance, one corner of his mouth twitching up into a smirk. "Of course, Ruler."

Turning and walking away was the hardest thing I'd ever done.

I'll investigate the new laws, Sequoia sent, sounding as furious with herself as I was with me, on the move from the feel of her power. *How did I miss this? I'm sorry, Ruler. I've let you down.*

You haven't, I sent, riding the elevator up a floor to my quarters. *Let me know what you find out. I need to uncover what's been done and how.*

I almost collided with Elphremantic as I stormed from the platform and into the hallway. The slim, handsome demon caught me carefully, spinning me sideways with a concerned look on his face. I shivered at the contact. While he was now the most likely candidate for my mate, I still held out hope for Rameranselot and found it difficult to fully accept the advances of the kind young demon before me. To his credit, Elph had as yet to push his case past my willingness to consider him and was, instead, one of the shoulders I leaned on these days.

My present irritation must have been clear to him. His dark hair hung over one eye as he frowned in worry.

"Are you well, my Ruler?" I'd spent the last week or so getting to know him better and, though he finally agreed to call me Meira in private, he continued to address me as Ruler in public.

As it should be, Ahbi groused.

I shook my head, at both of them. "I'm fine," I said to Elph, even as I shot, *Stay out of it*, to Ahbi.

"I've just found out your grandfather has replaced Jabut as guard captain." Elph walked with me to my quarters, hurrying to keep up as I stomped my progress forward, long, black jacket flaring out around me. "Is Jabut hurt or incapacitated?"

"Neither," I snarled as I slammed my door open and stalked into my suite. "How did you learn of this?" Especially since I'd only just found out.

"Word is making the rounds," Elph said. "I'm sorry."

His contrite attitude didn't help my present state of mind, knowing everyone was likely now aware Henemordonin had succeeded in undermining me even further. My aide, Pagomaris, rushed forward to assist me as I discarded my coat and turned to find Sassafras had returned to my quarters. "Sass, what the hell happened?"

"I have no idea," he said, hunched on the edge of a chair with his fur standing on end. "We've been careful to keep an eye on Henemordonin, but we've missed something."

I paced, hands clenching and unclenching at my sides. "We thought we were winning," I said. "But it would seem I've failed yet again." I sank into the chair next to Sassafras and uncurled my fingers long enough to stroke his fur. "How could I have let this slip through?"

"Is it possible he's lying?" Sass looked up at me with his whiskers hanging low.

There is that, Ahbi sent. *But he has to know he'd be caught.*

I nodded slowly, biting my lower lip. "Henemordonin would never take the risk of lying outright," I said. "So, however he managed it, he's passed laws without me."

That's it, then, Ahbi sent. *The First Seat is now impotent.*

I wanted to snarl at her, to attack with an angry retort.

But I had none to give.

Because I feared very much it was the truth.

"Don't be such a downer, Abhi," Sassafras sent with so much confidence I immediately felt buoyed. "Sequoia will find the answer. But, in the meantime, we need to find a way to corner Jabut and talk to him."

"We'll have no chance of that," I said, "if Rutorith has any say in the matter."

Just kick him over the side of the mountain, Ahbi sent. *Problem solved.*

Elph hovered nearby, finally speaking up as I rolled my eyes at my grandmother's blasé murder offering.

"I think I can help," he said. "Give me a few minutes." He disappeared out the door before I could stop him or ask what his plan was. And, before I could even think to go after him, Sequoia reached for me.

Ruler, she sent, mental voice urgent. *Jabut is leaving. You have to act now.*

chapter three

The elevator was just starting to move when I leaned over the edge of the platform rim and grabbed it with my power. Several demon guards, Rutorith among them, looked up at me with startled expressions. I was relieved to see Jabuticabron in their midst, his weary face none the less eager to see me.

As the platform came to a halt, I shoved the guards aside with power and slipped a shielding of magic around my former captain, pulling him toward me. Rutorith's hard-edged face darkened, but I shoved him back with more energy.

"There is no law," I said, "keeping me from talking to him, is there?"

Rutorith looked like he wanted to say otherwise, but when Elph came to a thundering halt beside me, slightly out of breath and waving a piece of parchment, the fight

19

seemed to run out of the old soldier—at least, on this issue.

"According to law," Elph panted, "Ruler may question any demon she wishes for as long as she wishes, as long as that demon is present to be questioned." He rattled the page again. "No law counter," he added.

The writing on the parchment flared amber, proving he spoke truth. Had there been a counter law, the words written there would have flared red.

Rutorith took long enough to give in, but he finally shook his head. "The law must be upheld," he said, as though it were the only thing that mattered.

Interesting, Ahbi sent.

I didn't answer her, not caring at the moment what the old soldier thought about anything. "Excellent." I set the elevator in motion, watching the guards drop to the floor below. "He'll be with you presently." I sealed off the entrance to my floor and spun to face Jabuticabron with a sharp exhale of relief. "Are you all right?"

He bowed deeply to me, face twisting in guilt. "My Ruler," he said, voice choking in the back of his throat. "Forgive me, I tried everything I could to reach you."

I shook my head as he bowed his. It was easy to feel him tearing himself apart inside. I sent him energy, supporting him and showing him how happy I felt just to see him. Jabut lifted his head, wiping his mouth with the back of his hand as he shuddered.

"Come," I said, leading him toward my office. "We have to talk."

Why, Abhi sent, softly and curiously, *did Henemordonin let us win this one?*

Sorry? I guided Jabuticabron past his former guards, Sassafras scampering forward while Elph closed the doors firmly behind him. *Win?*

Sequoia slipped into the room through a small door at the far end by the windows, her anxious face falling to near-grief as she rushed toward her brother. He hugged her gently, whispering into her hair while Sassafras leaped up onto a chair and pawed at them both, purring so loudly it muffled Jabut's words. They opened their arms to their furry brother, Sequoia scooping Sass up to hold him between her and their massive sibling.

I let them have their moment, turning instead to Elph. "Thank you," I said.

He bowed to me, handing over the parchment. My eyes widened as I scanned it. "This is an order for a restock of the kitchen," I said.

Elph winked. "But Rutorith didn't know that."

I erupted in laughter, my hand shaking as I handed the page back to him. "Sneaky," I said. "I think I'll keep you."

Elph's cheeks reddened. "It was all I could think of," he said, setting the page on the top of my pile of signed documents. "I'm glad you approve."

His skin was warm under my hand when I squeezed his fingers in mine. His earnest, open face, his willingness to help, only made me sadder about the loss of Ram to the Planeless. While Elph's kindness was welcome—a rarity in a demon—I missed Ram's steady confidence and support, his sense of humor and the way he made me feel like no matter how much power I possessed, he would always see me for who I really was.

I turned from Elph and sank into my office chair as I remembered the conversation Ahbi began.

Mind telling me what you're talking about? My fingers toyed with my pen to keep them busy. *What do you mean, he let us win?*

She sighed. *Done with your little flirtation, are you? Ready to focus on the important things?*

My jaw jumped, teeth squeaking as they ground together. *He helped us, didn't he?* Her dislike and mistrust of Elph was getting tiresome. He'd proven himself to me more than enough. But he would never be enough for Ahbi.

Just forget it, she snapped. *And focus. You've missed the obvious. Again.*

She was about to earn herself a quick trip out of my head if she wasn't careful. *Stop being a bitch, Ahbi*, I sent. *I'm so over your attitude.*

My grandmother huffed, but finally got to the point. *Henemordonin didn't have to question Jabuticabron in his office.*

She tsked softly. *Honestly, Meira, that boy makes you slow to catch on.*

I didn't snap back this time as I sat up straighter in my seat, hands dropping to my lap, eyes locked on the siblings now turning to face me after their little reunion. *This was a setup of some kind?* I stared with growing unease at the three offspring of two powerful demons.

Or a show, Ahbi sent. *He's finally ready to challenge you.*

My hands fisted around the skirt I wore, slick plastic-like fabric quickly heating under my grip. *Let him. I'm ready.*

You're not, she sent. *None of us are. And Henemordonin just proved it to you.*

Jabut turned from Sequoia, though he kept one arm around her shoulders as Sassafras jumped down onto the surface of my desk. He sagged, not the powerful, confident demon I'd sent to protect our people, but looking very young and very troubled.

"As soon as I began to fulfill my orders," he said, "Henemordonin blocked me. I tried to reach you so many times," Jabut's fist struck his hip as he spoke, "but I was unable. It was a matter of hours before I was demoted and Rutorith took my place. I was certain you had nothing to do with it."

I nodded my head to confirm. "I had no idea," I said. "I've been trying to contact you, too." *I should have pushed past Henemordonin's block,* I sent to Ahbi, guilt eating at me as I looked into the hurt and confused eyes of Jabut, wishing, not for the first time, Ram was by my side. I missed his steady presence so much at times like this, the way he would watch me with his confident gaze, steer me away from temper and toward decisiveness. He would have known what to do, I was sure of it.

Ahbi chose to ignore my mental wishing, focusing on the present problem. *You did what you could*, she sent, her abrupt about-face not making me feel any better. *Let it go and focus.*

"When I finally demanded an audience with you, he told me the new laws took away my right to do so." Jabut shook his head. "It's a tenant as old as Demonicon. Any demon can ask to see Ruler, no matter their standing." I didn't know that. "When I was denied, I knew something horrible had happened, but I had to follow my orders."

"You did the right thing," I said. "I'm just glad to see you're all right."

He bobbed a nod. "Thank you, Ruler," he said.

"Question," Elph said. "One you've asked, my Ruler. Where are these new laws coming from?"

"They can't be legal." Pagomaris hovered next to me, eyes huge and sad.

"They are." Sequoia looked suddenly hurt. "I'm sorry, Ruler, but the new laws are real."

"What did you find out?" I leaned toward her, disrupting a pile of parchment at my right elbow. I'd

24

signed so many things in the last few weeks—

With horror, I followed Sequoia's gaze to the stack and stared at it as though it would bite me.

Too late, Ahbi sent. *I think it already has.*

"Each law was enacted by Henemordonin," Sequoia said. "And seconded by a member of court. But they have all been duly signed." She hesitated before slumping. "By you, Ruler."

I pushed back from the desk, tipping over my chair. "Impossible," I said. "I scan every one of these before I sign them. I'm not stupid." Did I miss something? Nagging doubt rose and flourished. Did I really do this to myself?

"No one is saying you are," Sassafras said even as Jabut's jaw jutted out.

"They'd better not," he rumbled, fire back in his eyes. "Or they answer to me."

Sequoia softly patted her giant brother's arm. "It's all right," she said, meeting my eyes again. "I'm happy to hear that, Ruler. Which means, someone is forging your signature, or..."

"Also impossible," I said. "I can see how they could manage my handwriting, but how would they match my power?" I paused. "You said either. What's the 'or'?"

She nodded. "Or, someone has access to the power of Demonicon and is using it to ratify laws."

No one spoke for a long moment as we all processed

the truth of this situation. There was no question who this "someone" was. And now I understood why my grandfather hadn't been pushing me so hard, lately. And why he'd allowed me to lull myself into a state of confidence and optimism. Henemordonin had figured out a way to enact law and apply my approval without my knowledge.

"How many?" I almost didn't want to know, but I really needed to.

Sequoia shook her head, tiny bells in her hair tinkling. "I don't know," she said. "I've only just uncovered the truth. But, from what I've seen, there could be hundreds." She gestured in the air beside her, the image of a vast repository appearing as a holographic picture. I'd only visited the law archive a few times in the last four years. "The newest laws are filed by age," she said, zeroing in on the massive shelf climbing toward the darkness above. In the vast room, demons scuttled like beetles among the stacks. The place always gave me a headache when I entered and even now, just from the three dimensional representation Sequoia summoned, I felt my temples tighten. I frowned past the budding pain as the bottom four shelves began to glow. "These have, as yet, to be filed," she said. "There are over a hundred of them." I gaped at her before she held up both hands in haste. "Not huge laws," she said. "More like tiny cuts. Little bits and pieces of rearranging."

26

"It makes sense," Sassafras said, calm and cold as Sequoia allowed the image to fade and vanish. His level tone helped settle me somewhat. "Larger changes would be noticed immediately. But small things, inconsequential things, would be a perfect test for him, to see if he could get away with it."

And now, Ahbi sent, *he's ready to act.*

How do you know? I hugged her as she went on, hugging me in return, our previous spat long forgotten.

Because he let you talk to Jabut at last, she sent. *There's no other explanation. He wants you to know he's beaten you.* She hesitated and then continued. *That he's beaten us.*

"I'll deal with Henemordonin," I said, not sure how, but knowing I had to do something and immediately. I'd tried so hard to be clever, to play his game. But, in the end, he'd proved to me I wasn't half the manipulator he was. Which meant I had to find a new way to fight. Instead of pushing that idea, I turned to Jabut. "An update, my captain, on the Planeless."

His shoulders stiffened, face losing its harried edge. "Ruler," he said, saluting. "They have gone to ground, as far as we can tell. I must report, however, more demons join their ranks every day, though we are unable to find out how or track them in time to stop the conversions."

I'd had enough, up to here, over the top and around the bend. I was already moving before anyone could stop me, though they wouldn't have succeeded.

My grandfather was going to be the end of Demonicon if I didn't stop him right now.

CHAPTER FOUR

Meira, Sassafras's mind snapped in mine as I stormed my way down the hall toward my grandfather's office, *you have to keep it together.*

I've been keeping it together, I snarled back. *A tactic which has gotten me nowhere.* I'd traded Rameranselot's sardonic but gentle guidance for the snappish and familiar whip-crack of my demon cat. I don't think either could have slowed me down, no matter the influence the two had over me. The power of Demonicon crackled around me as I stomped my way toward the small gathering of guards outside Henemordonin's door. *Time for some confrontation for a change.*

Ahbi's anger boosted my confidence, but I couldn't suppress the soft shiver of old fear, four years in the making, winding its way up my spine. I was about to face down my grandfather and endure him yelling at me.

You can do it, Ahbi sent. *I'm with you.*

And that was the biggest difference this time around. It used to be Ahbi and I were as much at odds as myself and Henemordonin. But now that I had my grandmother to back me up, I was not about to allow him to intimidate me into silence and submission.

That's my girl, Ahbi sent. *Now get in there and kick his demon ass.*

The guards at the door didn't try to stop me. I suppose that should have been my first warning sign, but I ignored their sudden willingness, including the growing smirk on Rutorith's face, and stormed through the doorway, my magic preceding me.

Something is very wrong, Ahbi sent even as I came to a breathless halt at the top step leading down into the main room. *Meira, we need to be careful.*

Understanding mixed with shock as I took in Henemordonin's altered office. It used to be packed with ugly black furniture and hideous paintings of angry-looking demons, all previous Second Seats Henemordonin admired. Gone were the thick, shaggy pelts of *xyaltil* that once hugged the floor in their musty heaviness, and missing was Henemordonin's significantly gigantic desk, easily twice as big as mine.

My breath caught as I took in the new décor before me, even more so when the fifty or so demons standing at the foot of a throne dais turned to watch my reaction.

A throne. Henemordonin sat on a throne at the far end of his office, hands steepled before him, staring at me without a hint of guilt while the gathered demons—all members of my court—remained silent and watchful.

Ahbi panted her sudden fury in my head, but I didn't need her anger to tell me what was going on here.

"YOU DARE!" The power of Demonicon burst from me, a corona of flame rippling outward, singing the tall ceiling, sweeping forward over the hasty shields erected by the gathered demons. Traitors, all of them.

Henemordonin's power pushed back against mine, his wards parting the flames and sending them past him to flicker out. "You are not welcome here," he said.

"THIS IS MY DOMAIN!" I knew I had to pull back on my temper, absolutely had to regain control. But with Ahbi feeding me, the monster inside me woke and demanded I drain my grandfather to the dregs of his magic. Right. Now. "YOU WILL STAND DOWN."

"I will do no such thing." He waved at me as though I were insignificant, an irritating fly. "And until you end your little temper tantrum, none of us will acknowledge your presence further."

They turned away from me, some grinning, some scowling, the members of my court. While the full complement was missing, there were enough I knew I was in serious trouble. Fully a third of the family was in cahoots with my scheming Second Seat, and who knew how many more, though unwilling to show their hand just yet?

Meira! Sassafras's mind broke through my growing panic. *Pull it together or get your ass out of there. Pick one.*

How? How could I possibly do either when he sat there, my grandfather, on a throne. In front of my court. Making laws behind my back.

"If you're through being a hysterical child," Henemordonin said while the rest of the gathered demons tittered and whispered, "you may approach."

Ahbi exploded inside me, but Sassafras was faster. I don't know yet how he managed to block her off from me, but when she erupted into a nuclear blast, I was shielded from the full brunt as my demon cat slammed hard against me.

Meems. The anger was gone from his mental voice, all of his worry and fury faded. *You have to pay attention.*

"Second Seat." Elph's voice startled me, soft but carrying across the space, "your pardon, but our Ruler has the right to demand answers."

"Indeed," Sequoia said from my other side, piping tone sharp with sarcasm. "She is, in fact, Ruler. Perhaps you would deign to share your situation with the demon who carries all the power of Demonicon."

That made them sway, the court traitors, though Henemordonin simply frowned. Perhaps he expected me to arrive alone, without backup. If that were the case, I might have an edge after all. And with Sassafras holding Ahbi at bay, I was able to shake free of the stunned, cold feeling holding me still and start thinking again.

"Not all the power of Demonicon," my grandfather said with cryptic contempt.

"I would know the nature of your meeting." Of course I already knew while my power sniffed around his. It couldn't be, I carried the magic of Demonicon with me, as Ruler. I was well aware his only intent was to undermine me and take control of the government, but he couldn't do that without access to the power I carried. How had I missed his covert attack on me? Or the fact his magic now carried the same weight as that of the plane's combined energy.

Probably because he kept everything so public, Sassafras sent. *We thought we were seeing all of his effort. Obviously, we missed a large piece of the puzzle.*

Two large pieces. I pulled back on my magic, still stunned to find he'd stolen power from me at some point without me noticing. Henemordonin sat back in his throne, crossing his legs. "I am running this plane," he said, "something you, Ruler, have proven too untried and young to succeed at yourself."

Says who? Ahbi's rage had faded from a volcanic eruption to a bubbling caldera of fury.

How did we not sense this? I threw the question at my

grandmother though I took equal responsibility.

He hid it well, she sent, still smoldering. *Damn him to the deepest pits of hell. He's been planning this for a long time and only now is willing to show his hand because he has enough support he knows we can't defeat him.*

My stomach contracted in response, though as I writhed inside, searching desperately for an answer, I wasn't alone in trying to stand up to my grandfather.

"I beg to differ," Elph spoke up. "Ruler saved us from the cult known as the Planeless."

Gratitude woke, but only reminded me yet again of Ram and who I wished defended me.

"She's done nothing of the sort," my grandfather said, a snort following his words. "She's instead created a conflict where one doesn't exist, committing our forces to a chase after ghosts and illusions all out of fear." He leaned forward, jabbing a thick finger at me. "And a Ruler must be fearless in all things."

The court members murmured their agreement, though I noticed not so many of them were willing to meet my eyes this time.

"Perhaps if I had the support of my Second Seat," I said, Sassafras keeping my voice level with a surge of power, "this issue would have been resolved without having to resort to sending out our forces. Forces, I might add, who have reported the Planeless continue to expand their numbers despite the illegality of such an action."

Excellent, Sassafras sent. *More of that and less of the screaming and yelling.*

I didn't respond as Henemordonin seemed to relax further, despite the sudden nervousness of the traitor court.

"Lies," he said, almost happily. "Spread by a guardsman demoted for his falsehood, a creature created by Ruler meant to undermine the trust demons have in their government."

Mabel can't have him, Ahbi snarled. *I'm going to haunt him for the rest of his miserable life.*

I ignored her, again with Sassafras's help. "According to you," I said, holding my trembling hands tight against my sides as I fought for control. "But we only have your word for it, don't we, Second Seat?"

I don't think he was expecting me to be rational. Perhaps part of my grandfather's plan was to wind me up so tight I did his job for him. Again, he underestimated the power of having friends who truly cared for me.

But my continuing challenge was only a minor victory. My grandfather shrugged, hands folding in his lap. "As we only have your word."

Time to change tactics, Sass sent. *Ask about the laws. And the stolen power.*

"It's come to my attention," I said, dropping my voice a few notes to hide its shaking, "many laws have been passed in secret, laws I have had no part in creating."

Henemordonin gestured to the gathered court. To a demon, they had the courtesy to look briefly guilty. "These laws are for the safety and protection of all demons," he said, smooth voice rippling with honey and reasonable kindness, a sickening shift from his arrogance even the court he'd appropriated seemed to find hard to swallow. "You yourself, Ruler, passed a law allowing me to handle the smaller, more minute details of governance, a task I've taken on whole-heartedly." He scowled at me, disappointment clear on his face, vibrating in his voice. "And now you judge me—judge us," he again pointed toward the traitor court whose shoulders straightened and expressions hardened, "for doing our due diligence?"

I did no such thing, I spluttered.

Oh, but we did, Ahbi sent, deflating, bitter. *Remember? We decided to let him handle the little things while we take on the big things.*

But he's chosen to push that boundary, Sass sent. *You gave him the opening, Meira. You too, Ahbi. Damn it, you should have known better.*

We all should have, I sent, knowing I was beaten. There was nothing I could do and from the smiling benevolence hiding his true thoughts shining on my grandfather's face, he was enjoying the fact I only now understood the truth.

I had one small piece of ammunition left, though I

was certain he could counter it, too.

"And when, I ask you," it was so hard to keep the bitterness from my voice, "did I give you permission to steal power from me?"

I was right. His smile just deepened.

"I don't know what you're talking about," he said. "The signatures on those laws are mine. And the power comes from that of this court." The demons swayed, nodded.

This I didn't expect, Ahbi whispered. *He's created a second Demoniconian core.*

He's what? I almost jerked in denial. *He can do that?*

Sass's sad mental voice hummed softly. *Oh, dear.*

Ahbi's misery spiraled inside me. *Meira*, she sent. *I'm sorry. We're done here.*

I could have stood there and argued the point until Demonicon fell, but I had lost. Instead of giving my grandfather the satisfaction of hearing me rant and rave, reinforcing the lies he'd obviously been telling his pseudo court about my instability, I turned and left, shards of dignity and power trailing behind me.

chapter five

"He's not done," Sassafras spit, fur standing on end as I re-entered my quarters, Sequoia closing the door behind us. "There's only one reason he would create a second core of magic. He's after First Seat."

Of course he was. We knew that all along. But I never really believed he would succeed before. Now? The real fear he might actually depose me burned like bile in the back of my throat. I stood there in the middle of the room, hands tightly clasped to my chest, heart pounding so fast and so hard I was certain it would leap out of me and crash to the floor. It took everything in my power to hold still, to keep myself from flying apart into a million pieces, to force my chest to expand and contract, breathe in, breathe out. A tunnel of darkness closed in around the edges of my vision.

I had no time for a hysterical breakdown, but one was imminent and I didn't know if I could hold it at bay. Or if I wanted to.

"How did he do it?" I felt the angry crackling of the magic of Demonicon as it reacted to my helplessness. "I thought the core came from all of the planes, all demons."

"It does," Sass said, slumping onto a cushion with his ears sinking to the sides. "He hasn't made a full core, just a reasonable facsimile. All he needed was the support and sacrifice of a sliver of magic from each of his followers and he had a ready-made source."

"And with that support—backed, we can only assume, but most of the court—he's managed to circumvent the need for you to sign law into reality." Sequoia shivered, hands rubbing her arms as her face crumpled briefly. "What can we do?" Her voice broke through my panic attack, echoing in my ears as I turned my head ever so slightly to see her wringing her little hands in real fear. "We have to stop him."

"We can't," Sassafras said, grim tone deepening his voice, though his fur settled into a more normal sleekness and his face lost its horrible sadness. "Outside of killing him, that is. He's cut your feet out from under you, Meira." I could barely see his glowing amber eyes through the black threatening to drive me to a full faint.

The only thing keeping me upright, even as my knees

swayed beneath me, was the hideous feeling of failure rising from the tips of my toes to engulf me. I tried to swallow, my throat closing over the effort, nostrils flaring to gain more air. Ahbi was no help, her raging distant in my head. I know I wobbled, only because my left knee snapped as it popped back into locked position, shaking my whole body.

The black tunnel vanished with the motion, a deep breath drawn into my lungs even as my friends rushed to me, Jabut reaching me first. My guard captain guided me carefully to a seat, hovering over me while Sassafras leaped into my lap, Elph sitting on my right side, Sequoia settling into a puddle of her vast skirts at my feet. Pagomaris hovered in the periphery, making small, helpless, squeaking noises.

I knew exactly how she felt.

"Maybe he's right." My voice emerged oddly calm despite the renewed panic swirling inside me. "Maybe I should just let him rule and be done with it. I'm obviously not up for this." I met Sass's amber eyes as his tail thrashed, whiskers drooping. "If I was, he would be long gone. But I'm no match for him, am I?" Sass didn't comment, head hanging. "It's the demon way. And I lost."

"No." Elph took my hand. His felt incredibly hot compared to mine, my fingers tingling as though they'd been frozen. "He is less a ruler and more a bully. Do we want that kind of demon on First Seat?"

Ahbi flinched. *Low blow.*

He wasn't talking to you, I sent. "You're referring to demonocracy."

Elph's face lit up and he nodded. "You are the perfect demon to lead us into our new way of being," he said. "You aren't just a demon, but a witch, with a unique skill-set. If we can only rid ourselves of Henemordonin, a new and bright future awaits all demons." Elph's face fell. "Forgive me," he said. "But your grandfather has to go."

Time to challenge him, Ahbi sent.

Sequoia's face scrunched, adorable doll-like features tightening. "That is the old way, Ahbi," she said. Only then did I realize my grandmother was speaking in everyone's minds. "You must find a way to use the new laws against him."

"We tried that," I said. "He's too smart for me." With too many years of experience undermining others. "And now he can do whatever he wants." Maybe he couldn't enact any huge laws yet—surely he hadn't gone that far. But the day was close I'd find myself deposed and the magic of Demonicon ripped from me by my own grandfather.

I thought I could handle him, Ahbi sent, soft and regretful. *I'm just getting in the way.*

The kindness in me wanted to comfort her, but I just didn't have the energy. I felt suddenly drained, as though

Henemordonin had done far more than humiliate me and undercut more of my ability to act. It was as if he'd actually taken the power of Demonicon from me already.

A quick touch—unnecessary considering I'd only just felt it—reassured me that wasn't the case.

Yet, Ahbi whispered.

And therein lay the fear.

"You wanted this," Sassafras said. "Are you going to just give up?"

"That's not fair," Elph said, pulling me closer to him, arm slipping around my shoulders. I welcomed his touch even as Sass glared, sparks falling from his fur to expire on my skirt.

"Fair won't make this any better," my demon cat said. "Fair, in fact, got us here in the first place."

He was right. "So now I stoop to cheating and betrayal," I said even as I pulled away from Elph. "And become my grandfather in the process."

No one spoke.

"Thank you." I stood abruptly, dumping Sassafras on the floor. "I just want to be alone for a while." The silver Persian hissed before shaking himself and turning his back on me, fat tail swaying over his rump as he made his exit into my bedchamber. Sequoia sadly went after him while Pagomaris led Jabut toward my private dining room. Only Elph remained and, as much as I would have liked to keep him at my side, I really did just want to be by myself.

He hesitated until I waved him out. With a quick nod and a half-hearted reach for me, he turned and followed Pagomaris, closing the door behind him.

I spun toward the balcony and stepped out into the light breeze the shielding let through. My eyes watered as I stared out over the city of Ostrogotho, my heart aching, the need to sob choking me while I clenched the railing tightly in both hands and contemplated my next move.

Terrible timing had me at a disadvantage as my sister chose that exact moment to reach across the veil for me. I spun in place as she tore open the rubbery membrane between planes and stepped through. One of my hands rose of its own accord to press to my trembling lips as Syd emerged from the dark basement back in Wilding Springs and crossed into the bright sunlight of Demonicon.

She took one look and rushed to hug me, arms wide. I stumbled as I fell back from her, knowing if she touched me at that moment I would crumble and break. That I would beg her to fix everything or to take me back with her where life was simpler, where I could just be Meira again.

Syd's arms fell, her face collapsing from worry to sadness. "Meems," she said.

Even her voice had a powerful impact on me, as much as her empathy. "Syd." I gasped her name.

"That bad?" She sat on one of the massive chairs placed around the small table where I sometimes ate dinner. Bless her, she leaned back, arms crossed over her chest, ponytail swinging over one shoulder.

I shuddered as I sank down across from her, holding myself as rigid and still as possible. At least the black tunnel hadn't returned, though I could feel the need to give in and pass out hovering in the background.

"That bad," I whispered.

Syd held as still as I did, not speaking, just watching me. She said once she believed in me, that I was a Hayle witch, raised for power. I believed her at the time, mostly because I needed to more than anything. But now, I wasn't so sure she was right.

"Henemordonin," I choked out, "is smarter than I am." It was almost as hard to speak those words as it was his name. "He's used my attempts to outwit him against me and created the means to write new laws without my approval." My teeth caught my tongue, blood from the cut hot in my mouth. "He's created his own source of Demoniconian power, Syd, the means to Rule. He'll be coming for me, next. And I have no idea what to do about it."

Syd grunted as though I'd punched her in the stomach. "Simple fix," she growled. "Let me know when you're going to kick his ass so I can get a swing in, would you?"

I ground my teeth together. "I don't think you understand," I said, focusing on her arrogant stupidity which made it easier for me to maintain my calm. "The laws are changed, the rules are different now and he has everything he needs to destroy me."

"Challenge him," she said, blunt and unforgiving.

"I'll lose." And that fact was the hardest to speak of all. Even Ahbi held her tongue, so I knew she agreed with me. "He has the support of the court." Enough, anyway, he was able to maintain law-writing power. "I'll be stripped and he will be undisputed Ruler of Demonicon."

Syd's foot began to bob on the end of her crossed knee, her face creasing in frustration. My sister wasn't very good at hiding what she was feeling, never had been. And to her, acting first and counting the bodies later was second nature. But she didn't understand this wasn't the kind of situation she could fix with posturing and threats. And I didn't have the energy to explain that to her.

"We've had this conversation," she said. "I can't afford to have Demonicon in trouble right now." She uncrossed her legs, sitting forward. "I'm still dealing with the mess Gabriel made." I could see it, then, the weariness in her face, how the line between her eyebrows—the same one Mom had—tightened and deepened as she frowned. Her cheeks were paler than usual, a sure sign she wasn't sleeping. "If you can't clean this up, I need to take action."

I stared at her, anger mixed with hope, though I was oddly happy to feel anger won. At least I hadn't quit entirely. Still. Did she just threaten to act without me?

Oh no, she did not, Ahbi snarled.

Syd rubbed her face with both hands before falling back against the chair with a heavy sigh. "I'm sorry," she said. "You're Ruler, I know that. And it's not easy for you. But, Meira, it's not going to get any better if you don't do something."

No, it was going to get worse. "You think I don't know that?" My voice chilled even me, it was so cold.

Syd's anger flashed in her eyes. "I'm trying to help."

"I didn't ask for help." A tiny part of me cried, begged me to pull back, to stop this growing tension between Syd and I. I did need her, I always would. But she picked the worst time to tweak my already damaged ego and I couldn't help myself.

When she sighed again, I wanted to slap her. A wall of fury rose from within me, all the hate and vitriol I felt against my grandfather burning me as I gathered myself to tell Syd to go away and never, ever come back.

Only to be stopped, my attention diverted as Pagomaris staggered onto the balcony with a cry of fear.

Syd and I both shifted our attention to her, my sister guiding the gape-mouthed demon aide to a chair as Pagomaris gasped a breath. She lunged for me, grasping my hand, squeezing it so hard I almost cried out myself while my aide slumped in fear.

"Ruler," she moaned, "Nunaresh is gone!"

CHAPTER SIX

Sassafras bounded onto the table before I could think of a response.

"Gone?" He pawed at Pagomaris while the others crowded close at the balcony door to listen. "What do you mean, gone?"

She shivered, releasing my hand with a guilty jerk. "Dark," she whispered. "As if it's no longer there."

I shuddered in turn, brain firing to catch up with this new development. "Tell me how you know," I said.

She wiped at tears on her cheeks, her flawless makeup making tracks down her skin. "My sister," she gasped. "I tried to reach her, just now. But I can't find her anywhere."

"That doesn't mean an entire city is gone, Pagomaris," Syd said.

My aide shook her head, violently enough her

headpiece sagged free, the conical metal swaying back away from her face. "I searched the entire plane," she said. "When I couldn't make a connection, I tried government offices, the homes of other friends and family." I didn't know Pagomaris was from Nunaresh. How did a demon from the free city end up aide to the Ruler of Demonicon? Even Ahbi felt shocked as Pagomaris went on. "Nothing, no one." She snuffled, hands shaking as she swiped at her tears. "Ruler, the city is either under complete lockdown—though I felt no shielding—or my fear is true and it has somehow vanished."

I stood immediately. At least this I could do something about. The communications panel in my office was only a short stalk down the corridor. I ignored the guards standing at attention at various points, though I privately wondered how many of them my grandfather owned.

I didn't bother closing the office doors behind me, leaving that to the others. Syd strode just behind me, as though giving me space, and I was grateful for it. I stopped next to the panel, selected Nunaresh from the cities available, and pressed the button.

Nothing. Only blackness stared back at me. I tapped power into the control panel, thinking perhaps Henemordonin somehow sabotaged the device, but it was in perfect working order. Though private mental communication was now allowed—one of the few laws I enacted myself—it was still easier to simply contact my governors from the com panel rather than using personal power to reach them.

I selected Bilhaeder and watched as the large display wavered with amber fire before a startled young demon's face appeared before me.

"R-r-ruler!" He backed away from the console, a few other demons behind him scrambling as he did. I didn't call very often, after all.

"Never mind." I hung up on him, hands settling on the panel before me before I punched the key for Nunaresh again.

"They could have just cut you off," Syd said softly at my elbow. "They are a free city, after all."

"No," Jabuticabron said, deep voice troubled. "The control panels are fed directly from the Node. If there was anyone to reach in Nunaresh, the device would work."

That gave me pause. I turned to him, his huge body slumped forward as he watched me.

"You're saying it won't connect if there is no one to answer?"

"No, my Ruler," he said. "It should connect if Nunaresh is there at all."

"Meira." Sassafras's fur bristled as he came to my feet. "You have to check it out."

50

"I'll go." Syd turned, the veil tearing under her magic, but I stopped her, my power between her and the gap.

"No," I said. "I'll go."

I was already moving, racing for my office door, when it slammed wide. Henemordonin burst in, mouth open, chest expanded as I shouldered him aside.

"Nunaresh is dark," I snarled on my way by. "Your crap can wait."

I felt his shock and realized then he already knew and had come to tell me himself.

To gloat, Ahbi sent.

We have to find out what's going on, I sent to the sound of my sister yelling at my grandfather in the room behind me. There wasn't much Syd could do to him aside from killing him herself, but it was nice to know she'd tear a strip or two from him while I dealt with this crisis.

I didn't know I wasn't alone on the elevator until I turned to find Elph panting behind me. Sassafras hovered on the edge of the platform, staring down at us as we descended the few flights to the transport bay. I opened my arms and the shields and the silver Persian leaped, my magic catching him and guiding his furry body into my arms. We both glared at Elph, arms crossing over my chest to support Sassafras as the demon held up one hand in supplication.

"I can't let you go alone," he said with so much feeling in his voice I sighed.

"Very well," I said. "But you realize if there is some kind of attack happening, you're putting all of us at risk if I have to focus on protecting you." The elevator came to an abrupt halt, one I was ready for and he wasn't. I caught him as he staggered, straightening him up even as I pushed past him and into the bay.

"I won't be trouble," he said, right behind me. "But you need someone to watch your back."

"That's what I'm for," Sassafras snapped, but didn't argue.

The transport attendants backed off as I commandeered a two-person flyer, the hull sleek and thin. I needed maximum speed and the smaller the vessel, the more I could cushion us against the G-forces it would take to reach Nunaresh as quickly as possible.

I felt Elph settle beside me even while I raised the shielding and rose from the floor of the transport bay. We were already breaking the sound barrier before I left the shelter of the Seat, the crack of our passing, I'm certain, shaking loose a few chunks of the mountain.

There was a time flying free was a joy to me, escape from the grinding pressure of my role as Ruler, from Henemordonin's constant manipulations. But not today, and, if this ended badly as I feared it might, maybe not ever again.

I pushed myself as hard as I dared, the surface of Demonicon flashing away beneath us as the tiny transport raced toward Nunaresh. Elph didn't speak , his own tension adding to mine while Sassafras perched in my lap, his front paws on the side of the hull, gaze locked on the outside of the vessel.

I knew where Nunaresh was. I'd been there several times for small diplomatic matters, though usually surrounded by a mass of Guards. So when we passed the grassy savannah that marked the border of Ilogabon and the free city failed to rise into view, I faltered.

The transport slowed in response, coming to hover over the empty expanse of rocky tundra below. Where once a mighty city had stood.

"It's gone." Elph's face paled to light pink. "It's really gone."

I nodded, unable to speak.

"There's no hole or crater," Sassafras said, tail striking me as it thrashed, ears twitching while his eyes scanned the surface. I lowered the transport to within feet of the ground, staring out over the harsh, blank rock. "And no gash in the veil." He shook his head, falling back into my lap, astonishment clear in his voice. "It's just…"

"Gone," I said.

This is impossible, Ahbi sent. *I want to try something.*

I opened to her, not able to resist through my shock as she reached for the Node.

I felt it through her, the vibrant and happy touch of the power holding the planes of Demonicon together. It didn't seem disturbed in any way, merely quiet and almost meditative. I exhaled, relieved to know everything was all right. It wasn't until Ahbi gasped I realized not all was well.

I don't feel it in the network, Ahbi sent.

Feel what? I was still a bit punch drunk, I hated to admit.

Nunaresh, she sent. *Pay attention.*

Her admonishment was enough to trigger my temper and snap me out of it. I followed her power, felt for the city. And came up as empty as she had.

That's impossible, too, I sent. *It can't have just vanished, Grandmother. The Node would be destroyed if one of the planes went missing.*

And yet, she snapped, *that's exactly what's happened. Feel it.* The difference was minor, but it was there. Nunaresh was a large city, yes, but the plane it existed on was small. Still, the Node felt reduced, smaller.

Demonicon is shrinking, Ahbi sent. *Nunaresh isn't the first plane to vanish.*

She was absolutely right. The reduction in volume was obvious, now I knew what to look for. Again, small and hard to spot without understanding what I was trying to find, but clear now I did know.

How did we not sense this happening? The Node's balance was a delicate thing, keeping all the gathered planes of Demonicon together. From what I knew, any disruption would mean the end of all. The almost surgical removal of a few planes shouldn't have been possible.

I don't know, Ahbi sent. *But we need to find out. Henemordonin may be a pain in the ass, but this takes precedence.*

To coin my sister: Duh.

CHAPTER SEVEN

We were almost home when the familiar sight of a drach soared through a gash in the veil over Ostrogotho and settled in to keep pace with the transport. I'd already been in touch with Syd, filling her in on the absence of Nunaresh, and could only assume she'd called in support in the form of the dragon-like first race.

The massive drach could be one of two, I figured and, when Mabel's mind touched mine, I was oddly happy to realize it wasn't Max who'd come to Syd's call.

I understand your troubles have increased, the drach female sent to me as I sailed into the transport bay and jerked us to a halt, cushioning our stop with shields. She shrank as she landed on the shining stone floor, flowing from her drach shape into a tall, broad woman with dazzling diamond eyes and a blank expression on her gray-skinned face. I leaped from the transport as it settled, shields dropping the moment we touched down, and went to her side. I'd missed her, more than I thought I would. We only spent a few short days together, but I found having her with me suddenly bolstered my damaged courage.

"Mabel!" I hugged her on impulse, feeling her arms around me, hearing the soft humming from her chest as she greeted me in turn.

"Ruler," she said in her rumbling voice. "It is good to see you well."

"And you." I stepped back from her, clearing my throat as emotion stirred. "Thank you for coming to help."

"Max would have come himself," she said, "but he discovered a further pocket of damage in the veil and was forced to deal with it personally." Mabel bowed her head to Sassafras as the silver Persian pawed at her foot. "Greetings, Sassafras."

"Mabel," he said, "Nunaresh is gone, as are a few other small planes. How could that have happened?"

Leave it to Sass to remind me there were more important things to consider than my aching heart.

She frowned, a dark expression, her skin flowing outward into a dragon's muzzle. It was as though she was unable to prevent the reaction. When her face smoothed back into human shape, she shook her head, thick, black ponytail sweeping over the ground.

"I do not know how such a thing would be possible."

Mabel's diamond eyes locked on mine. "Ruler," she said. "Come."

I followed her without question to the edge of the bay, not a zing of ego or a moment's hesitation holding me back. She leaped into the empty air, hovering in her human form, extending her hand.

"We must enter the veil," she said, "and find out what is going on."

I took her hand eagerly, leaving Sassafras and Elph behind. "Tell Syd," I said to the pair over my shoulder as Mabel's body expanded and transformed back into drach shape. I landed on her shoulders, power anchoring me to her back as her huge wings swept through the air, carrying us forward and into the sudden rent in the veil before us. Mabel let out a long, sorrowful cry as we passed through the gash and into the darkness beyond.

Syd often spoke of riding the veil, of being in control of where she went. I never had that experience, though I often longed for the ability. When I passed through the veil, I simply saw darkness, felt the slick, rubbery surface of it, and arrived at my destination. But riding Mabel into the thick black was an entirely different experience all together.

My fear, she sent to me, her vast mind touching mine gently despite the concern I felt in her, *is that the damage done to the veil has somehow harmed Demonicon's connecting planes. If that is the case, I must summon Max immediately. But* we must first investigate to discover if Nunaresh is damaged in any way.

How? My magic felt muted in the veil, dulled, but still present. Ahbi had been silent since we left the place where Nunaresh should have been and I felt her, as quiet as our power, watching and listening in the background when Mabel spoke.

The veil connects all planes, she sent, swooping over darkness. The occasional flicker of light rose through the black, though nothing I saw clearly, and again I wished for Syd's ability. *If Nunaresh is whole and well, we will be able to study it and find out why it has parted from the rest of Demonicon. There.* She back-winged in the dark, her magic rising in a rainbow of light to engulf me. *You see it?*

I did see, a network of connecting lines in a multitude of colors, stretching further than my eye could perceive.

This is the veil, Mabel sent. *Not a single barrier, but a massive, Universal network between all planes in this existence.* She pointed with her snout toward a red-tinted area far to our right. I could just make out flickering, flying things circling it. *That is a sample of the damage done to the veil*, she sent. *And those are drach attempting repairs.*

I gasped, chest tight as I realized just how huge the network was.

Yes, she sent. *Your planes are only a tiny fraction of the vastness of this Universe we inhabit, much as the Universe on the other side of the rift has its own multitude of planes, all connected by the veil holding things together. And yet, much rides on you and your sister, Meira Hayle. Fate has chosen this place, this time as the hinge point of choice. Sydlynn has completed the first stage of her task. But she is not the only one who needs to fulfill a task to maintain balance in the Universe.*

Me? My mental voice sounded squeaky even to me.

Mabel laughed, a rich and wonderful sound. *Take heart*, she sent, so gentle I bit my bottom lip so I wouldn't sob into the dark. *You are vital. And you are up to the task. Now*, she spun, *let us see what we can see.*

She dove suddenly, and though there was no up or down in the veil, I felt a strong sense of vertigo as she plunged into the black.

There, she sent. *I've found it. But, how odd…* She trailed off as we dove through a rent in the veil and out into soft sunlight.

I was so accustomed now to the multi-sun glare of Demonicon it seemed dim to only have one star above. But I barely noticed, drawing a thankful breath at the sight of Nunaresh, intact and glowing, far below. The entire plane appeared fine, undamaged, much to my relief. Demonicon might have been a collection of planes all sewn together with magic, but each individual plane, it seemed, hadn't lost its ability to survive on its own even after all this time.

So it's not gone, I sent.

No, she answered. *It is.* She hovered in the air above

the city. *Nunaresh is again its own plane.*

I choked on my response, my relief long gone. *Is it the damage from Gabriel?* I would hate to think my nephew had done so much hurt to our veil, no matter it wasn't his fault in the first place.

No, Mabel sent, tone thoughtful. *This is something else entirely.* She arrowed toward the sky so quickly I grasped onto her flesh in fright. The veil welcomed us again as she swept her way through it. *I have alerted Max,* she sent as another gash opened and we soared into the familiar light of Demonicon, the Seat towering beside us. *We must talk this through and decide on a course of action.*

What's happening? I slipped from her shoulder as she landed in the transport bay once again, my feet hitting the floor.She flowed into human shape next to me to the gaping stares of the attendants.

"I don't know," she said. "But until we find out, I fear Demonicon is at great risk of coming apart at the seams."

chapter eight

Syd paced my quarters, coming to a halt as Mabel and I swept our way in.

"What the hell is going on?" She nodded to the drach who nodded back. "Where did you go?"

"The veil," I said. "We found Nunaresh."

Pagomaris sagged with a soft cry. "Thank the Node," she said.

"It is no longer part of Demonicon," Mabel said.

I was prepared for the gasps of shock from my gathered friends and forged on. "No matter how much of an arrogant ass our grandfather is," I said to Syd whose scowl told me she'd lost their argument, "we need to tell him what's going on."

"What we need," Sass said from his perch in Sequoia's lap, "is for you to retake control and find you a new Second Seat."

"What makes you think Henemordonin will listen?" Syd's anger only grew, a visible glow in her eyes as she started pacing again. "For all we know, he's involved."

"But how?" I'd already considered the fact he might be somehow in bed with the Planeless leader, Xeoniteridone, but had discarded that idea even as I discarded this one. "And why? Syd, of all people, Henemordonin loves power. Why on Demonicon would he ever be part of something reducing that power?"

She stopped pacing and growled under her breath. "Gotcha," she said. Her eyes lifted to Mabel. "This isn't Gabriel, is it?" There was so much hurt in her question I wanted to hug my sister and comfort her.

The drach gestured, an image of Nunaresh safe and sound appearing between them. "There is no damage to the veil," she said. "It is simply severed from the Node."

Syd sagged slightly, relief replacing fear. "Thank you," she said.

"I'm going to talk to Henemordonin," I said, turning to the door. "You're all welcome to come."

I caught Elph's eye as I opened the door. He smiled at me.

"Ruler," he said. "I knew you were the perfect one to lead us."

I tried to absorb the positive energy he sent me, leaving the room with a slightly lighter heart and my confidence patched together by need and support.

63

It didn't take long to track down my grandfather. He sat in Second Seat, in the throne room at the top of the mountain, the gathered court waiting for me. I knew it left me in a weakened position, the fact he was there, waiting and ready, while I hurried to play catch up. But I didn't care. The safety of our collective planes was at stake and, by the Node, he was going to listen to me.

"Ruler," he said in his booming voice as I trotted up the stairs and spun to sit on my throne, "we've been waiting for you."

"Second Seat," I said, using the exact same tone he did, "I've been investigating a new threat to Demonicon and only now have returned from the veil." The court stirred, concern rising, though, from the skeptical look on my grandfather's face, he had plans for me.

Crush him, Abhi sent, still sullen. *And be done with it.*

"Again with your young and foolish panic," Henemordonin said, no longer looking at me, gesturing out toward the court. "And this is the demon you choose to Rule you?"

Meira. Syd's mental voice cracked like a gun shot.

I'm handling it, I sent. "Nunaresh," I said, "is gone."

That shut them up, at least for a moment. Henemordonin looked shocked, as though knowing the city was dark hadn't led him to imagine the truth. He masked his surprise with a frown quickly enough.

"Nunaresh has gone dark," he said, finger waving at

me in correction. "They obviously have finally taken the last steps of rebellion toward Ruler—"

"Nunaresh," I cut him off, sweeping to my feet, "is GONE." I gestured myself this time, showing them the place the city once stood. And again, this time the single and lonely star shining over the solitary plane Nunaresh inhabited. A gratifying round of gasps and soft squeals of fear raced through the court while Henemordonin spluttered in his seat.

"Lies!" He stood himself, though the dais steps kept him below my height still. "Deceptions by a pathetic and weak Ruler bent on controlling us with fear!"

I almost spoke, though I didn't have to. Not when Mabel strode forward, turning to face the court with her back to me, her drach form shimmering around her on a small scale as she spoke.

And Henemordonin thought he had a booming voice. Hers shook the shields around the peak of the Seat, made the very stone beneath me vibrate as she raised both arms, the image of the interior of the veil appearing as if we were really engulfed in it.

"RULER SPEAKS TRUTH." I swayed as the three dimensional image drove us toward a crack in the veil, much as we'd done when I rode Mabel through the dark. "Nunaresh exists. But it is no longer a part of your collective."

Henemordonin staggered below me when the image

died and Mabel turned to stare up at me.

"It's not possible," he whispered.

"And yet, Second Seat," Mabel said, voice quieter though still rumbling with power, "it has occurred. I myself have explored the rift, at the behest of your Ruler. She and I witnessed it firsthand. Nunaresh is no more of Demonicon."

Shouts of, "How?" and "Why?" and other equally unhelpful questions rose in a wave from the gathered court. I glared at my grandfather, his pale face, how he swallowed hard past his fear. When his eyes met mine, I saw the depth of his terror for a moment and knew he would be of no help to me whatsoever. My understanding was reinforced the moment his fear shuttered over with returning arrogance.

He pointed at me, hand shaking in righteous rage. "What have you done?"

"You will not blame her for this," Mabel said, silencing him and the rest of the court instantly. They stared at her, mute and terrified even as my grandfather sank into his throne. "Some force attacks the integrity of your collective. You must act, or Demonicon is doomed to once again break apart into small planes unable to support themselves."

Henemordonin opened his mouth, some horrible response ready to fly, only to fall silent as the room shook slightly. This time, I felt it when the Node shifted, almost a hiccup. We all did. Mabel's head cocked to one side as the world settled again.

Meira, Ahbi's panicked voice gave me goosebumps.

I strode down the steps to Mabel's side. "If you would join me," I said, "I would visit the Node monitors and discover the truth of this."

Heavy footsteps followed behind me, Henemordonin's power pressing against me as he joined us. "I will go with you," he said, grim tone angry. "To ensure it is not, in fact, some ploy of yours to regain control of our people."

I didn't bother to respond. Instead, I accepted Mabel's hand, Syd at my side, Henemordonin hovering behind me, and stepped through the gash in the veil the drach opened.

If the Node monitors were surprised to see me, they didn't react that way. The lead monitor, Sharrapelle, appeared almost instantly as we entered the control room. I'd been here a few times. The first I barely remembered, still in the clutches of nectar addiction. But thanks to Dad—and yes, this was one of the few things he did right—I now had free access to the Node and the monitors, Ameline Benoit's attack making it apparent more oversight was necessary.

"Ruler!" Sharrapelle bowed deeply to me, smiling and gesturing for me to enter the monitor station. I glanced around at the few monitors watching over the readings

PATTI LARSEN

spread on a circle of panels and felt a chill. "How lovely
for you to visit."

"You have no idea, do you?" How could they not be
aware of the loss of Nunaresh? And, if Ahbi was right, a
few more planes as well?

Her smile faltered, faintly wrinkled face pale as her
gaze flickered to Henemordonin and back to me again.
"Idea of what, Ruler?"

"Don't look at him." I stepped into Sharrapelle's face,
pushing against her with a surge of energy. "Has he
ordered you to keep threats from me?"

Sharrapelle spluttered, backed off. "My Ruler," she
said. "I would never!"

Liar, Ahbi hissed.

Irrelevant now, I sent. "The Node is in danger," I said.
"Several planes have gone missing from the network. And
you mean to tell me you haven't detected anything
wrong?"

This time, her defensiveness seemed genuine. She
drew herself up, skinny shoulders sharp under her
uniform. "I can assure you, Ruler," she said with a nod to
my grandfather, "if anything were amiss with the Node, I
would know about it."

She really believes it, Ahbi sent. *We have to explore for
ourselves.*

I pushed past Sharrapelle and headed for the center
of the room where the veil could lead me to the Node.

68

Henemordonin made a loud protest behind me. I turned to see Mabel standing in his way, Syd backing her up. The drach nodded to me as Henemordonin's power slammed against hers while my sister laughed.

"Nice try," she said as I stepped through the veil tear I opened. "Just push me a little harder and we'll see if Meems needs a Second Seat when this is over."

I grinned into the coolness of the next chamber as the veil sealed behind me. Though there were times I worried about Syd's impulsiveness, I adored her sense of fair play.

My amusement stilled as Ahbi sighed softly inside my head, shrinking in on herself and going quiet.

Grandmother? I stepped closer to the large, teardrop shaped Node, its soft amber light casting over me in the circular chamber. The stone walls here were dark, but not the same black stuff I was used to. My eyes skimmed over the rough walls, to the hollow in the floor over which the Node floated. It felt serene, welcoming even, reaching for me.

No, not for me at all, but for Ahbi. It touched her gently, kindly and she shuddered away from it.

It's fine, she sent. *I just... Meira, there's something very wrong here.*

The Node suddenly wobbled on its round bottom, the air around us rippling with power. I felt the core exhale, and, because we were right there at the moment, actually experienced the exit of a plane in real time.

Ahbi choked out a cry while I stumbled back as the flow of power making up the plane broke free and washed over me in a rippling flow of amber sparks. The Node shivered softly before settling again.

Why didn't it fight? I was still trying to get my balance from the feeling of hundreds of demon souls passing over me when Ahbi spoke. Her anger wasn't aimed at me but at the Node itself. *It just let the plane go!*

I touched the Node's power with my own, reaching for it with the magic of Demonicon and felt a sudden chill. My power felt thinner, reduced.

Of course it does, Ahbi sent in a crackling tone. *With every plane we lose, the magic of the combined plane is broken down into its component parts. If this keeps up, not only will Demonicon be fractured again, there will be no Ruler and no power*. She grunted. *Not even for your insufferable grandfather.*

The Node whispered calmly its gibberish while I stared at it helplessly.

If it doesn't know it's in danger, I sent to my grandmother, *how can it protect itself?*

It can't, she sent.

This is insane. I walked to the edge of the gaping hole and reached out physically to touch the side of the Node. The power engulfed my hand, softly pulled on me, drawing me in, but I resisted, dropping my hand. *There's nothing wrong here, and yet…*

And yet. Ahbi sighed out her anger and fear. *Someone*

has figured out a way to split the planes so precisely the Node not only remains it balance, it almost willingly gives up that which it's meant to maintain.

But why? I hugged myself, the creaking vinyl clothing I wore feeling suffocating. *To what purpose? Demons are all about more power. Why would anyone want to reduce it?*

To make the planes vulnerable? Ahbi's tentative answer left us both with more questions.

It makes no sense, I sent. *But, at least we found out before too much has been lost. We need to shield the Node so this doesn't keep happening.*

Agreed, Ahbi sent. *Though, might I remind you, this place is as shielded as any on Demonicon.*

Then we pour all we have into it and hope it's enough, I sent. *And if it isn't, we have Syd and Mabel shield it, too.*

Ahbi didn't feel very optimistic, but, at the moment, it was the best we had to work with. *Quickly!* She pushed against me as I felt the sigh of the Node begin again. The magic of Demonicon rose in a rush, surrounding the Node and protecting it in a flaming ball of power.

We might as well have held a sieve under a tap. I shuddered as another tiny plane left the collective, only a handful of souls departing. I sagged as my magic retreated.

This is terrible, Ahbi stated the obvious. *At this rate, there won't be a Demonicon in a matter of weeks.*

Can you talk to it? She'd lived with it for a while. Surely the Node would listen to her if she told it about the danger?

Might as well have a conversation with a rock, she sent. *It understands basics, Meira. But if it doesn't sense trouble, there is no trouble.* A heavy sigh escaped her. *Want a lesson in futility? Live with the Node knowing it has the immeasurable power of multiple planes of existence and the cognitive power of a newborn puppy.*

Then I have to correct your assessment of how much time we have, I sent, weary all of a sudden and unable to muster fear. *If we don't find a way to stop it, Demonicon has days.*

CHAPTER NINE

I emerged into the monitor station with a heavy heart, to find Mabel waiting for me, but noting my sister and grandfather were gone.

"Sydlynn took Henemordonin back to Ostrogotho," Mabel said. "By force."

I nodded. "It's bad," I said. "We felt another plane leave, but couldn't stop it. The Node is coming apart in slices and there's nothing I can do about it."

Mabel's hand touched my shoulder, the contact bringing my sagging head up. "We will find out the truth of this," she said. "And we will save your planes."

I wished I shared her confidence. I led her through the veil to the Node. It greeted her with some enthusiasm, though it almost felt sleepy to me. We'd talked, before the present mess made my life a different kind of hell, about how Ahbi and Syd had changed the

Node. How their presence had altered it somehow. That deep quiet I'd sensed earlier was a different one than what I'd felt when Ahbi mentioned the changes she and Syd made to the core of Demonicon's power through their influence.

When yet another small hiccup rose in the Node, I stood back and let Mabel's power flare. And though hers managed to slow the exodus, I still had to live through the same shuddering experience of the souls of demons leaving Demonicon.

"Baffling," Mabel said. "And most troubling."

We returned to the monitor station where Mabel contacted Max. I let her do what she needed, focusing at last on the internal problems I was having with my monitors. When I met Sharrapelle's eyes, my anger returned.

"You," I pointed at her chest, "are no longer in charge here."

She gaped at me, thin body beginning to tremble. "My Ruler!"

"Clearly, you don't consider me such," I snarled. "If you would allow Second Seat to bypass me."

She shivered as Mabel turned to glare at her. "Shall I dispose of her for you, Ruler?" While the drach weren't a violent race, despite their appearance, I'd seen her temper and though I assumed this was a false threat to support me, I didn't want Mabel to crisp the cringing demon just

74

yet.

"We shall demote her instead," I said, "for a first infraction."

Sharrapelle fell to her knees before me, profuse thanks lost in a sea of blubbering. I turned away from her, eyes scanning the other monitors, falling on the face of a young, lovely demon woman who stared openly back.

"You," I pointed to her. "Your name?"

She came directly to my side, bowing, sidestepping her now prone former leader. "I am Aniseop, my Ruler," she said.

"You will take her place." I turned to Mabel who nodded and opened a gash in the veil. "You understand communication is vital?"

My new monitor leader nodded quickly. "We have all worried for some days now," she said, "that there was an issue with the Node." The rest of the monitors joined her head bobbing. "But Sharrapelle insisted all was well and you knew of the trouble."

"Clearly not the case," I said. "I trust I can count on you to keep me informed?"

"Absolutely, Ruler," Aniseop said. "We shall begin a thorough investigation immediately."

I strode through the veil with Mabel, wishing it would be enough, but knowing, for now, there was nothing more we could do.

Mabel delivered me directly to my room, hovering a

moment over Ostrogotho before dropping me on my balcony. I waved to her as her mind touched mine.

I must speak to Max directly, she sent. *I will return.* And, with that, she flew upward into a slash in the veil and was gone.

For a long moment I stared over my city, fear for its survival making me feel weak. Though Ostrogotho would be fine, as the sight of Nunaresh's intact state proved, how would demons survive without Demonicon as a whole? The point of the assembly of the planes was to give demons a chance to develop culture and creativity.To save them from the basics of existence they endured, unable to access the raw materials they needed to move past subsistence living. Millennia of development and outlawing more deadly battling had made a massive difference. The demon race had become able to advance well past their humble and violent roots. Would my people survive without the infrastructure we'd all built together?

I looked up at the many suns spiraling overhead, all the stars of each plane bound together here, on this one created to support our race, and wondered how many of those had left the sky already.

My boots made a soft grinding sound as I turned at last and entered my room, finding Sassafras and his siblings waiting for me. Elph stood to one side, his relief at seeing me safe clear on his handsome face. I nodded to him while Pagomaris shakily rose from a seat even as I waved her down again.

It was short order to give them the details of what I learned. I had just finished with Mabel's failure when the air beside me shimmered and Bakari appeared. Perhaps I should have been angry with him for taking such liberties, but instead I greeted him with more calm than I think I should have felt in that moment. Considering the grand sum and total of my rule so far was a massive failure and pending Demoniconian doom, I felt I was holding up quite well.

Too well? I was a Hayle, after all. Perhaps threats—not just strife—were necessary to trigger my inner strength. If that were the case, I had the distinct feeling I was going to be very strong indeed before this was all over.

"Ruler," the assassin said, bowing his head to me, frown telling me he'd overheard the conversation. "Grim news."

"Grim indeed," I said. "Tell me you have better to share regarding the Planeless."

He shook his head, regret genuine despite his rock-like expression. "Our people are baffled," he said. "There isn't a corner of Demonicon where they could hide from us, and yet we have turned up no sign of either Rameranselot or Xeoniteridone." He glanced sideways at Pagomaris who dabbed at her cheeks with a lace handkerchief. "I fear my son is lost to the cult."

His—

His what?

Bakari's eyes darkened, the normally deep amber dropping to a burnt orange. "I had kept this from you," he said, "but my superiors believe maintaining such deception is now detrimental."

His—

"Ram is your son?" Sassafras managed to speak long before I could. Speaking wasn't possible. Neither was breathing, not when my feelings were suddenly twisted sideways and squeezed until I ached.

"He is," Bakari said while Ahbi blew a gasket. "Investigating the Planeless was not his job. But my son has always been impulsive."

I THOUGHT I COULD TRUST HIM. My grandmother's mental voice was so loud even Bakari winced. *Rameranselot was nothing when I found him. I took in a stray, taught him, trained him—*

"Ahbi Sanghamitra," Bakari said with a growing smile, "you have been had."

She stopped yelling abruptly and cursed. Black washed over me even as my limbs tingled while I returned from shock. Her anger fed my kindled resentment, the hurt in my heart so powerful I almost choked on it. Or choked Bakari. I had that option standing in front of me, though harming him would do me little good.

Ram's reticence made total sense to me now, through the haze of my heartbreak. He never cared about me, not really. I was an assignment. How clever and convincing of him, to make me love him so easily, to pretend to be there for me when I needed a shoulder, all for the sake of making sure I was doing my job.

"It was the best way to watch over you," Bakari said, his words cutting through the bitter fog of darkness trying to suck me dry, "making you think taking in Ram was your decision."

When my heart finally stopped weeping, I shook my head with a sigh drawn from the depths of my feet, acceptance easier than clinging to despair. Didn't I have bigger things to worry about right now? Silly Meira. He's just a boy. Get over him and move on. Still, I couldn't resist a shot at his father. "I shouldn't be surprised, should I?"

Bakari just smiled. That fired up my rage again, Abhi's, too, and if it hadn't been for Sassafras's interruption, Bakari might have found himself squashed to the floor and begging for his damned life.

"Where is Syd?" I turned to Sass who shuddered, his silver fur rippling.

"She left a little while ago after dropping off your grandfather." His teeth flashed as amber fire flared in his eyes. "Neither seemed very happy. Syd said she'd be back."

"Mabel went to talk to Max." I stepped away from them all, turning my back on them. "For now, why don't we all try to get some rest?" I spun again, forcing a smile, as grim as it was. "There's nothing we can do until then." I'd already tried.

And failed.

I faced the balcony again, hearing them depart one at a time, though I knew Bakari could easily have remained in camouflage. It really didn't matter, not while I turned over and over what he'd told me and the truth wormed its way past my attempt to shove it aside and I finally accepted the absolute understanding.

Ram was of the assassin sect. Not who I thought he was at all. He'd lied to me from the moment we met and I never once suspected he was something other than the demon I had fallen in love with. A demon I now realized I knew nothing about.

I thought it was over already, the snap-crackle-crunching of my heartbreak. I'd never been so wrong. The wave of emotion now taking over was almost my undoing and, I think, if I had been alone after all I would have crawled under my blankets and not let anyone drag me out. To hell with Demonicon and my grandfather and the Node. I'd been through enough, thank you, to have to also come to terms with the fact the one I loved played me for years.

Drops of moisture fell from the tip of my nose as I

hung my head and silently wept. A hand touched my shoulder and I turned to face the owner, wiping at the tears I shed for the loss of my first love. Elph stood quietly, face sad, keeping a small distance between us but hovering close enough I smelled the scent of his skin, felt the soft exhale of his breath across my cheek.

"Meira," he said, hands rising, arms opening. "I'm here if you need me."

How easy it would have been to sink into his arms and allow him to comfort me, to weep further and, maybe, find a way to heal my heart in the beating of his. But if I'd learned anything in the last little while, I was a Hayle and I needed to keep moving forward, not collapse in on myself. What Elph offered was a further failure. I saw it clearly and, in a way, I was grateful to him for showing me the truth of the matter.

I hadn't failed, not yet. The only real way I could fail was to quit. Or to let Ram's betrayal break me. And that I would never permit to happen.

My fingers brushed his cheek and I smiled past the last of my tears. "Thank you," I said.

Elph must have seen my denial in my face because he smiled back before bowing to me. "My Ruler," he said. "I should never have thought you, of all demons, would need such comfort."

He turned on his heel and left me alone while I wished things could be different.

chapter ten

I tossed and turned, trying to get some sleep, wondering how I could ever sleep again knowing Demonicon was falling apart around me. But even I needed rest, lest my judgment become clouded by stress and worry as well as the expended power I'd used up in the last day or so.

It felt like putting everything on hold, lying there in my giant bed while the moons rose one by one through my window. And yet, I'd done everything I could for the moment, or, at least, I told myself so. I'd tried to reach Syd again just a half hour earlier, only to catch Sashenka in the basement when I opened the veil.

As the veil opened to the familiar family basement, Sashenka looked startled, hands full of candles. She squealed in surprise, dropping the heavy wax cylinders, catching them with the family magic just before they hit the floor.

"Sorry," I winced.

She laughed and tossed back her long, dark hair, spinning the candles into place with a burst of energy before shrugging her thin shoulders. Her exotic coloring always made me think of demons, not witches, though Shenka had none of my race's blood in her. Her grin was genuine as she approached the rift in the veil, expression warm and welcoming.

"Meira!" Shenka brushed wax dust from her hands as she smiled. Her white teeth flashed against the soft coffee color of her skin, dark brown eyes catching the light of the single bulb over her head. "Are you looking for Syd?"

"Hi, Shenka," I said, feeling rude all of a sudden. After all, the only times I ever saw Syd's second was when I had to see my sister. It's not that I avoided Shenka, exactly. But I was self-possessed enough now, at eighteen, to realize I'd done all I could to avoid Syd's best friend out of childish spite and jealousy.

You're growing up, Ahbi whispered.

"I know she's probably not home," I said to Shenka, ignoring my grandmother. "But I thought I'd check in just in case."

My sister's coven second frowned slightly. "No, she's not here," she said. "Max appeared a few hours ago after she returned from Demonicon. She's been gone ever since." Shenka paused before rushing on. "If you knew she would be, that means the trouble with the veil is worse than she told me. Isn't it?"

My shoulders lifted and fell as my body heaved a sigh. "You could say that," I said. "And a world-class mess unfolding here, too."

Shenka's brow furrowed. "I'm sorry," she said. "Can I help?"

That was Syd's second, and at that moment I understood why she was the perfect choice. I could never have stood in Syd's shadow. But Shenka didn't see it that way, not at all. Her absolute concern was so selfless I felt it even across the veil. Was I capable of putting others ahead of me like her? No, I wasn't. While I had no problem stepping up and doing what I could to solve problems, Shenka's temperament served in other ways, outside the spotlight.

Well, now, Ahbi sent. *It's an evening of revelations.*

There's nothing wrong with being a leader, I sent.

Agreed, Ahbi sent. *As long as you're aware why you want to lead.*

Shenka didn't interrupt our little conversation and when I realized she still stood, patiently waiting for me to answer, I laughed out loud.

"Used to this, huh?" She had to be. Syd and her multiple personality disorder had to have trained Shenka to wait until the internal dialogue ran out before prodding again.

Shenka's laugh warmed me and softened the edges of my fears, if only for a moment. "You have no idea." She rolled her eyes, but there wasn't a trace of malice in her tone. "At least you only have one other occupant. When Syd gets chatting with her demon, Shaylee, and the vampire essence... I might as well just go watch a movie and wait for her to work it out." She paused, smile fading, before she crammed both hands into her front pockets as though to keep from reaching for me. "Syd's not saying much," she said. "And you know what she's like, keeping things to herself until it explodes and she can't handle it alone."

Ahbi snorted. *She's talking to the pot to Syd's kettle.*

Oh, hush, Grandmother, I sent. "Feel you," I said aloud.

Shenka nodded. "So," she said, "be honest with me. I can tell something huge is going on with Max and the drach. But is there anything I should worry about?"

I laughed, not sure why, but letting it out anyway. "Feel free to worry," I said, surprised at my good humor considering my circumstances. "Won't do you much good, but..."

Shenka laughed, too, shoulders relaxing. "It's what I do best," she said. "Are you helping her? Because, if you are, I won't worry so much."

She might as well have thrown cold water in my face. "Why is that?"

Shenka tilted her head to one side, snapping her

fingers as she finally pulled her hands free from her pockets. "You Hayle girls," she said. "I just dare anyone to get in your way."

And can I get a hallelujah, Ahbi sent.

My cheeks flushed, and though my worries about the future remained, Shenka's point-blank trust and faith triggered the old family pride.

"You could say I am then," I said. "If it makes you feel better." The fact neither Syd nor I were working on the same problem at the moment didn't have to cross Shenka's radar. She had her own job to do, protecting the family. And Quaid would be busy watching the kids with Galleytrot's help, now that I'd stolen Sassafras from them. Shenka had enough on her plate than to worry about things she couldn't change. I waved to her, odd relief hugging me tight, the whole conversation a balm on my heart. "No more taking, 'I've got it covered,' for an answer. Have Syd fill you in when she gets home."

Shenka's teeth flashed again. "Oh, you better believe Ms. Sydlynn Hayle will have some explaining to do when she arrives," she said with a wink, "which she will, safe and sound. Like always. But if it's all the same, I'll worry about the both of you anyway. Just a little bit."

We said our goodbyes, the veil slipping shut between us. I was unable—and unwilling—to wipe the little smile from my face, savoring this small bit of happy for another moment while I reached out for my sister, on the off chance she was here, on Demonicon. When I didn't find her, my smile faded and I chewed my bottom lip, thinking.

She was probably in the veil with Max. Which meant out of reach. Or did it?

What are you thinking? Ahbi had this habit of being so quiet at times I almost jumped when she spoke up.

We can open the veil, I sent. *But do we have to open it somewhere specific?*

Hmm. Ahbi's own dark melancholy seemed to shift as she pondered. *Nice idea. That's how Syd rides, correct?*

Exactly. I reached for the veil again, focused on tearing my side, but with no particular destination. It didn't work, the power simply humming in front of me. So much for that idea. It had been clever enough I was certain it would work.

Don't give up so quickly, Ahbi sent. *So you can't ride the veil the way she can, between planes. But it doesn't mean you can't reach her.* Ahbi touched the still-hovering power awaiting my command. *Try focusing on your sister, instead of on a location.*

Brilliant, I sent, grinning, my happy mood after talking to Shenka still alive and well. *Let's try it.*

When I focused, I felt sure it would work. I think it tried to. But the tear didn't appear, just a wavering spot in the air in front of me before the magic retreated like a nervous dog unable to obey a command.

We're onto something, Ahbi sent. *We just haven't quite hit on it, yet.*

What's so special about Syd she's able to ride the veil? While there could have been bitterness in my question—and would have been just a few short weeks ago—I was honestly curious at this point.

She's maji, Ahbi sent.

But she's been riding the veil for a long time, I sent. *Long before she was maji. Back when she was still fighting her power. She had only her witch magic—as I do—and her demon's.*

Which means, Ahbi sent, *you should be able to repeat her success.*

I should ask her to teach me, I sent. *You were never able to accomplish it?*

Ahbi shrugged in my head. *Once*, she sent. *By accident. And it was so long ago, I barely remember. I was only a girl, around your age.* Her mind contracted a moment as she retreated into her memories. *But riding the veil was always forbidden, as much as draining another demon was against the law. Of course, I pushed those boundaries, but it never worked for me the way it does for your sister.*

Interesting. I yawned, my jaw cracking as a wash of weariness came over me suddenly, dizziness following. I pressed my hands to my temples to keep myself steady. *I'm too tired to work it out right now.* I sank to the end of my bed, the soft surface drawing me in. *I know I should do more, but…* It seemed a byproduct of my newfound moment of connection with Shenka was a final descent into sleepiness.

There's nothing more to do, Ahbi sent. *You were right. You need rest. Syd will alert you when she's back. Until then, you're not thinking straight and we need you clear headed.*

Which led me to lying, sleepless and tossing, in my bed. So much for my weariness. The moment my head hit the pillow, I was wide awake again.

Do you want me to sing to you? Ahbi's mental voice held no sarcasm. *I used to have a passing voice, once.*

Thank you, I sent, *but I guess I'll just get up and try to work.* That was the problem, though, wasn't it? Work at what? I couldn't just carry on with my normal routine while Demonicon was being shredded by some unknown force?

I think we both suspect it's not an unknown, Ahbi sent.

I sighed into the dark. *The Planeless. You think they are part of this?*

I know they are, she snarled, but not with anger at me. *It makes the most logical sense, Meira. All this preaching about peace and love, and yet they suppress the power of demons to do it. And what feeds the Node?*

Demon power. I nodded against my pillow. *But why? If Xeon is after power, which is the only thing that makes sense, how is tearing Demonicon apart serving him? It makes as much sense as Henemordonin being behind it. Demons call to power. They don't give it up willingly.*

Ahbi was silent a moment. *I don't know*, she sent,

clearly as exasperated as I was. *This is so illogical I can't wrap my head around it.*

My eyes drooped at last, and I released a massive yawn. *There's not much logical about the cult*, I sent.

Sleep, Ahbi whispered. *We'll figure it out after you've had some rest.*

I mumbled something in response as the darkness and quiet finally embraced me.

Ram's mouth brushed mine, his breath sweet, hot, the touch of his skin burning me as his hands pulled me against his bare chest. I leaned into him, biting his lower lip, sucking on the fullness of his flesh, my demon power flaring to life and in need.

You betrayed me. *I slammed into him with magic even as I pulled him tight, nails digging into the hard muscles of his shoulders, his back.*

I love you, *his mind roared* . And I have always been faithful to you.

Guilt drove me back even as anger rose, pouring hot coals over an already blazing fire. You were not! *No longer did desire drive me, but hate and rage so powerful I was consumed by it.* You lied to me. You never loved me. *Ram fell with a cry as my magic pummeled him to the ground, blood gushing from his nose and the lips I'd just kissed.* I hate you!

He died with a sigh, the light leaving his amber eyes while I fell to my knees and wept over him, begging him to come back to me—

MEIRA! I jerked awake from my nightmare, cheeks wet from crying, to the sound of Ahbi screaming my name.

I wasn't alone. A shadowy figure hovered over me. The dream lingered, my mind reaching, hoping for Ram, only to encounter another all together. My power flared, too late, as my attacker lunged.

CHAPTER ELEVEN

I half-fell out of the side of the bed, my shoulders hitting the soft fur as my lower half twisted in an attempt to dodge the shadow leaping toward me. The ball of amber fire I tried to summon died in a sigh of smoke even while the light weight of a female demon landed on top of me, pulling me the rest of the way to the floor in a puddle of bedclothes.

Shhh, Zinnia's voice whispered in my head. My father's ex-fiancé held my gaze with her bright amber eyes, face tight with concern. *Ruler, be silent.*

I stopped struggling, Ahbi's freaking out in the back of my mind making it difficult to focus. While Zinniaperimote helped me recently, warning me about my cousin, Tanasharia, and that demon's plans to challenge me, the last thing I expected was to find the stunningly beautiful female in my quarters in the middle of the night.

How did you get in here? I tried to push her away and found her oddly strong despite her slim build.

That doesn't matter now, she sent. *Please, you have to listen.*

Ahbi fell still, taking control of my body, snapping in my head. *Someone's coming.*

I didn't have time to ask her what she was talking about when the door to my chamber creaked softly open.

Zinnia slithered away from me, gesturing in the low light of the setting moons through the window for me to follow. I did without hesitation, staying as low as possible, glancing over my shoulder as another line of shadows entered the room behind me.

The normally flat and empty wall swung open, Zinnia's hands pulling me roughly inside a tiny space before she firmly but silently closed the panel behind her. I shook, the shock of such sudden activity after the twilight of sleep making me feel stupid and slow.

My night vision finally kicked in as Zinnia pointed toward the cubby's concealed doorway.

Ahbi should have told you this was here, my father's former fiancé sent as the sound of shuffling and whispers came from the other side.

My grandmother's spirit grumbled, but didn't comment as Zinnia and I both peered through the tiny cuts in the slats of the wall, the decoration hiding the thin slices exposing the room beyond. I raised one hand to shield the glow from my eyes, hoping it would keep the intruders beyond from spotting me and Zinnia nodded.

This side is tinted, she sent. *We're safe as long as they don't know this hiding place exists.*

Who is they? I dropped my hand, frowning, anger rising at last. *Why are we hiding?*

Just watch. Zinnia pointed again as the group of a half-dozen or so demons surrounded my bed, their shadowy shapes hunched forward. Black robes hid their forms, hoods pulled over horns and faces, making it impossible to identify them. Their hissing whispers carried, but not well enough, and when I tried to use magic to hear better, I was blocked by the same emptiness that killed my fireball.

I turned to stare at Zinnia in growing horror, taking in her grimace of discovery.

I can explain, she sent, hands open wide even as her sorcery held my power at bay. *Please, Ruler. I'm not one of them.*

One of who? I looked back through the slice in the wall's façade, just in time to see the moonlight fall on a familiar face I hoped I'd never see again.

My first cousin, the former Second Plane Princess Tanasharia, scowled as she spun away, she and the others hurrying back toward my door. I gaped in the silence of the hidey-hole, hands trembling. I pressed them both to the inside of the hiding place, feeling the vibration of my surge of fear transfer to the panel. But the group was long gone, too late to hear the soft rattle I raised or the sigh of relief Zinnia expelled.

Come, she sent, slipping the door open again. I didn't move, not until she turned with real concern on her face, gesturing to me. *I know you have no reason*, she sent. *But I beg you, Meira, trust me.*

Can we? I sent to my grandmother even while my body moved forward in response.

There is much more here than meets the eye, Ahbi sent. *I suggest caution, but we need information, too. And Zinnia has done nothing to make me think she's one of the Planeless. If anything, she's in opposition to them.*

She has sorcery. Zinnia nodded as I joined her, circling my bed to the other side of the room. *If she's not Planeless, then who?* A second panel opened in the wall between my bedchamber and my dressing suite. I walked through it, finding myself in the midst of my clothing, slipping past as Zinnia did to a further passage.

Possibly another faction, Ahbi sent. *One we know nothing about.* I expected her to be frustrated and angry. After all, she'd been Ruler for centuries and had no idea. The fact sorcery existed in demons and she didn't know about it had to be troubling her. My grandmother's pride wouldn't allow her to swallow this bitter pill easily. Instead, however, she seemed bemused and curious and not at all concerned for my wellbeing, a fact that put me strangely at ease. *How strange. I knew of the hiding place, but this is new to me.*

We followed a strange demon sorcerer who'd hid her power from us, fleeing the Planeless cult into a dark passageway, and all Ahbi could do was focus on the escape route?

These passages were created for those who watch, Zinnia sent, clearly hearing every word my grandmother and I shared. *I will explain everything. But we have to hurry.*

Three more passages and we stood in an alcove overlooking the city. It was so cleverly carved from the rock of the Seat mountain, I knew no one would find it without knowing it was there. Even I let out a startled cry when Zinnia seemed to step into thin air, only to find a narrow staircase wound down the side of the mountain, as well hidden as the alcove.

There are times magic is a detriment, she sent, *and your feet are your best friend.*

I stayed put, shaking my head. *I'm not going anywhere,* I sent, *until you tell me what's happening.* Truths clicked into place as I thought about my cousin's appearance in the dead of night in my bedchamber. *Tanasharia is one of the Planeless,* I sent, finally shaking off the last of my shock and disorientation. *I saw her converted.* My dear cousin turned me in to Xeoniteridone when I'd tried to spy on one of his recruitment drives.

She is, Zinnia sent, returning to my side, face grim. *Ruler, you attempted to stop me with magic. What happened?*

Nothing, I sent. *The fire died. You used sorcery.*

Ahbi listened silently as I held back the question I wanted to ask.

I did, Zinnia said. *And, as you are now aware, not all who do are in opposition to you.* She shivered, arms around her. I realized only then she wore as little as me, a thin robe over a revealing nightgown. At least I slept in a silken shirt and long pants and felt far less exposed than she must have. Regardless, the wind making it through the Seat's shields was cold enough to bite through the thin fabric.

So Tanasharia is a sorcerer, too? How had Tanasharia gained power over sorcery? My fears the Brotherhood— my sister's enemies—had come to Demonicon to take over rose yet again.

Her power has been awakened, Zinnia sent. *By the nectar and by the loss of her demon magic.*

You seem to know a great deal for a simple court demon, Ahbi sent as I struggled to process what she'd said, cynical and dry.

You, of all people, should know, Zinnia sent directly to my grandmother, *very rarely are things what they appear on the surface, Ahbi Sanghamitra.*

Why are you helping me? I took a step back as a stiff breeze pushed through the shields, unsettling my footing near the edge of the staircase.

There are those of us who believe you are the Ruler we need,

Zinnia sent, making me think of Elph. *We will not stand by and allow you to be taken over by the cult.*

Thank you, I sent. She nodded quickly.

We must go, she sent. *And again, though I know you have very little reason to trust me, I hope I've gained some from you. Enough you will come with me.*

I can't leave, I sent, entire body clenching against the very idea. *How can I just leave? I have responsibilities here.*

You are no longer safe on the Seat, Zinnia sent. *That much is clear.*

How did you know they were coming for Meira? Ahbi's suspicion sparked my own alive again.

Zinnia sighed heavily, out loud. *I don't have time for this*, she sent. *You can come with me now, Ruler, or you can wait for them to find you. The choice is yours.*

She turned and began to descend. I caught her three steps down.

I'll come, I sent, suddenly trusting her more than maybe I should have. *But we need to make a stop first.*

Zinnia frowned. *If we can*, she sent. *Where?*

The lab, I sent. *I need to talk to Theridialis.*

Zinnia finally nodded. *An excellent idea*, she said. *We can take him with us.*

I pondered this new twist of my fate as we navigated the tiny staircase, one hand slipping over the comfort of the cold mountain beside me, my eyes firmly fixed on the back of Zinnia's gown where her shoulder blades shifted under the thin fabric.

Where was Sassafras? He usually slept with me. His absence made me worry for him, though I wondered if I dared reach for him.

He's likely with Sequoia and Jabut, Ahbi sent. *Do not fear for Sassafras. He is very capable of taking care of himself.*

I need to let them know I'm leaving, I sent, panic making a soft arrival, my skin tingling from it and my head lightening until I had to force myself to breathe for fear I'd fall over the edge.

Zinnia halted suddenly, turning toward the stone face. Only then did I see the narrow space carved in the rock.

Amazing, Ahbi sent as I followed the demon woman through the crack. *I had no idea.*

That was the plan, Zinnia sent with a small measure of smugness.

Was the entire mountain laced with back hallways and secret doors? I could only imagine now that was true. After a short walk and three doorways through tiny storage rooms, when the last entry slipped open and exposed the lab, I found myself stumbling into the light with relief.

Pots and beakers bubbled, the scent of peppermint, cinnamon and chocolate in the air tweaking my nectar addiction. I hesitated, pulling together my calm even as I realized the vast lab was empty.

Zinnia hurried to the small room at the back where

Theridialis had been sleeping. She emerged a moment later, shaking her head with a grim expression.

"He's not here," she said.

"He may have gone back to his own lab." I gestured at the still-boiling series of concoctions he was working on. "He couldn't have left long ago."

Zinnia sighed, hands rubbing together quickly before she shrugged. "We'll check," she said. "We'll need him, I think."

Considering he was working on a cure for the nectar the Planeless used to enthrall demons, I agreed with her.

We could try to ride the veil. I hadn't figured out how yet, but I was willing to give it a try again. I pushed against it, but Zinnia shook her head.

"Not safe," she sent. *"Not with the disruptions in the Node."* Instantly I worried about Syd. Zinnia must have known where my thoughts went, because her full lips curved into a lovely smile. It was the first time I allowed myself to admit she really was a gorgeous demon. "Your sister will be fine," she said. "She has other powers to protect her, if you recall."

And a drach, supposedly. I nodded and followed again, feeling like a child hurrying after her impatient mother, still wondering if I should contact my friends and let them know what was happening.

Soon, Ahbi sent. *Let's see this through.*

And if it's a trap at the end? Even I didn't believe that.

So be it. Ahbi hugged me quickly, a tiny hint of excitement escaping.

Are you actually enjoying yourself? I almost spluttered, a grin on my face. *We're running from the Planeless who somehow managed to make it past all the security in the Seat with a demon we don't know for sure we can trust completely toward who knows what.*

I know, Ahbi sent. *Awesome, isn't it?*

chapter twelve

The descent took over an hour, at least, so by the time we touched down on the edge of the Parade at the base of the mountain, most of the moons had set and the first suns were starting to light the horizon. Zinnia pulled two heavy black robes from an alcove at the bottom, slipping her hood down over her face. I copied her, my bare feet slapping on the smooth grounds of the Parade. She skirted the edge, taking us into the city as soon as the perimeter gave way and permitted us to leave the wide expanse at the base of the mountain.

I usually took a transport to Theridialis's tower, though I'd ridden one of the public transit system trains with my sister in the past. I assumed we would do so now, only to raise my eyebrows at the small and dented, but fully intact, transport hull Zinnia uncovered behind a large panel at the back of a non-descript building.

"If it's all right with you," Zinnia said, settling into the tiny shell, "I'll fly."

I sat behind her, the only space available, and hugged my robe around me while my good sense warred with my need to trust her. "If you betray me," I said, "I'll kill you."

"I am well aware," she said as the shields snapped into place and the transport rose, "that you will try. Hold on."

We climbed into the lightening sky, Zinnia's power expertly handling the small craft. I usually loved the view over the city this time of day, but I couldn't bring myself to look at anything save the single tower of Theridialis's lab as it grew closer and closer. I wished she would hurry, though I knew we flew at speed and, by the time she settled the transport at the top of the tower, opening the shields for me to exit, only about a minute had passed.

She left the craft hovering, joining me as we hurried down the wide hall to the main lab. Theridialis's name was on my lips as we burst into the space, but my mouth froze open instead.

The destruction of the lab was absolute, the floor covered in shards of glass, twisted and blackened tubing, tables torn in two as though by the hands of giants, cast aside to splinter against the stone walls. Panic so powerful it suffocated me crashed down, making me stumble as I tried to enter. Zinnia held me back, shaking her head.

"You're in bare feet," she said. "And he is not here."

Her grimness did nothing to make me feel better.

"I have to call the others," I sent, my panic cracked, but still in control. "We need to find Theridialis."

Zinnia's quick frown told me what I needed to know of her opinion. "Ruler," she said. "What part of 'you're not safe' wasn't clear to you?" She gestured at the mess. "This just reinforces our worries for you."

I pulled away from her, feeling for the demon scientist. I searched as far as my mind could reach, seeking even a scrap of him, and came up empty. My next attempt at contact was for Sassafras, a little surprised Zinnia didn't use her sorcery to try to stop me this time. His mind met mine in a snap of power while I shook my head at Zinnia.

"I will not run," I said. "And whoever you represent must know that."

She slumped, her curvy body sagging in defeat. "He told me as much," she said, though the mysterious "he" remained unidentified as Sassafras's mind crackled.

WHERE ARE YOU? I felt him running, bounding in his cat body, his magic reaching for me.

I'm safe. I showed him the lab. *Your father is missing.*

He's in the Seat. Sass's own frantic fear eased as he slowed his pace. I caught a glimpse of Sequoia's worried face before he spoke again. *We just saw him for dinner.*

He's not, I sent. *He's not at the lab on the Seat and I can't feel him anywhere. Sass, he's gone.*

Stay there, he sent. *We're coming to get you. And you'd better have a damned good explanation for being out on your own, young lady.*

I laughed, unable to help myself, hysteria taking over. *I'm not a little girl anymore*, I sent.

You damned well are, he sent. *My little girl, forever and always. Don't move a muscle.*

Tears prickled my eyes as I let him go, turning to Zinnia.

And found she'd disappeared.

Well, that's just a treat, isn't it? Ahbi's irritation barely masked her continuing excitement. *Let's look around, since she decided to abandon us.*

Now that reason had taken over, I shook my head, thinking Zinnia hadn't exactly abandoned us as much as I'd rejected her offer for help. I just hoped I wouldn't live to regret it. I toed aside a small pile of glass and shivered when one sliver cut my skin. *I'd rather not ribbon the bottoms of my feet*, I sent, sweeping some of the shards aside with magic, though unwilling to destroy possible evidence I might miss in my present state. *We'll wait for Sass.*

It was a very long and very quiet ten minutes before anyone came. And all that time, my nerves turned to fear, then to anger and back to anxiety until I'd worked myself into a froth of emotion so strong, when Sassafras and his siblings burst through the door, I collapsed into sobs.

My weeping didn't last long, just a few gulping cries

to get my anxiety off my chest as Jabuticabron supported me, Sequoia hugging me tight, Sassafras between us purring so loudly my bones rattled. I stepped back after a handfull of barking coughs and pushed the tears from my face with angry hands.

A small number of guards stood in the doorway, staring. Jabut scowled at them and they quickly found something else to worry about.

I told my friends everything in hushed whispers while Sassafras snarled and spit and Sequoia gasped with her hands over her mouth. Jabut shifted from one large foot to the other, face downcast. I patted his arm when I was done.

"It's not your fault," I said. "The intruders had help." I'd come to that conclusion on the long walk down the mountain. There was no way the Planeless—sorcery or not—made it into the Seat and past all the protections without some kind of assistance.

"Not necessarily," Sass said. "They are able to travel through the veil, remember?"

I'd forgotten. My own slim confidence deflated as I realized the truth. "That means they can come for me anywhere, at any time," I said.

Which is why Zinnia was trying to protect us, I suppose, Ahbi sent.

"Who is she, then?" Sequoia shivered, rubbing my arm with one tiny hand. "We've all underestimated her."

106

"Does it matter at this moment?" Sassafras's tail was in overdrive. "This means demon magic really is useless in protecting Meira. Centuries of protections have no way of providing shielding. She's an open target to anyone with sorcery."

"We kind of knew that, my brother," Sequoia said ever so softly. "From the beginning, we've known, thanks to Sydlynn's experiences, demon magic can't counteract sorcery. No magic can." Her eyes met mine. "I think we've all been in denial about the issue, refusing to believe Ruler could be at risk in her center of power. But this has proved we've been lying to ourselves. The sorcerers' power outstrips ours. It's no wonder our guards fall to them whenever they have confrontations. Not only are they caught in the coercive spell of Xeoniteridone, even when they tried to fight," I caught Jabut's nod as his sister spoke, "their power had no impact on the Planeless."

I shuddered, though I refused to admit I obviously hadn't thought things through to the rational conclusion, too busy trying to counter my grandfather to think about the reality of my situation. Even Jabut nodded.

Ahbi wriggled in discomfort. *You, girl, are bad for me*, she sent. *Why didn't I realize?*

Maybe I'm affecting you as much as you're affecting me, I sent.

"We need to contact Syd," Sass said. "She's the only one who can protect you now." He sounded very disappointed, though I could only assume in himself.

"Zinnia seemed to think she and whoever she works for could do so," I said. "And there's Mabel." Personally, I would have preferred to have the huge drach woman at my side than Syd. At least she wouldn't overreact and yell at me for putting myself into danger like I was sure Syd was going to do.

"I want to know how Tanasharia developed sorcery all of a sudden," Sequoia said.

My stomach twisted as I thought it through. "Is it possible it's been there all along but we've never had access?" My mind shuddered and bent. If Tanasharia had it all along, could it be in all demons…? The concept grew massive in the growing panic of my thoughts.

Sequoia chewed her lower lip, tiny features dark with worry. "I don't know," she said. "We need to talk to Father." Her face collapsed then into sadness, though she hid it quickly.

"We'll find him," I said.

She nodded, tried a smile, and looked away.

I only hoped I could fulfill that promise to her.

chapter thirteen

We returned to the Seat and my quarters, Jabuticabron satisfied the guards he'd brought with him were investigating every last shard. I'd already toured the shattered lab with him, impressed by Sass's brother's ability to see things I missed.

"He put up a fight," Jabut said, pointing at Theridialis's favorite stool, one leg cracked and broken off, a bit of skin and blood clinging to it. "They didn't take him easily." Admiration shone in his deep voice. "Father always had a few tricks available that had nothing to do with magic." I followed his finger to the large black patch on the far wall, up near the ceiling.

"Explosive?" I sidestepped a pile of glass, cushioning my feet with power to keep me from cutting myself.

"A rather nasty one," Jabut barked a short laugh. "It's a solid until it strikes a hard surface, then turns to pellets that rain down. Each tiny drop is its own explosive." He rubbed his arms. "Very dangerous. He's never used it indoors before."

I could only imagine the kind of childhood Jabut, Sequoia and Sass must have had with a father who took innocent and excited delight in experimenting with things that probably should have been left well enough alone.

We turned up no evidence as to Theridialis's captors, but I was willing to bet, if the scientist used alternative means to his sizeable personal power, it had to be the Planeless or someone with access to magic he couldn't counter.

In other words, sorcery. I could only hope he was all right after all. On the way home, I had to believe whoever took him wanted him alive or we'd have found his body in the tower.

We touched down, the transport settling next to my balcony window and dropping us off before Jabut sent it away with the pilot. I wasn't about to stand around waiting to see what other disaster might come crashing down on me and headed immediately for the door and my office.

I didn't make it far. The air beside me shimmered softly, bringing me to a halt just before I collided with stone-faced Bakari. He didn't move to evade me, standing as still as a demon effigy, looking down at me while I stumbled to stop myself from running into his chest.

"A little warning," I growled, Ahbi echoing the sentiment.

"I'll do my best," he said and, though his voice was as cool and calm as usual, I thought I detected a hint of humor.

"I take it you're here for a reason?" All of this mess had given me a waspish temper, something I never had before. I wasn't sure I liked who I was turning into.

Bakari bowed his head to me, backing off a step when I refused to budge. I was Ruler, wasn't I? Like it or not, I wasn't going to let him push me around any more than my grandfather.

"I have convinced the leaders of my order to speak directly with you," he said.

Ahbi gasped in my head. *Meira*, she sent. *Tread carefully. But accept.*

I returned his nod, mind spinning. "I'm happy to receive them."

Oh, very clever, Ahbi sent. *But you won't get anywhere with that attitude, young lady.*

Bakari's lips lifted into a humorless smile. "I will bring you to them," he said.

Don't give in too easily, Ahbi sent, her mind surging with eagerness. *But this is huge, my dear. Huge.*

I sighed at her silently. *Grandmother.*

She flinched. *Sorry. You're in charge.*

That made me laugh out loud. Bakari's eyebrow

quirked, head tilting to one side as I chuckled my way around Ahbi's words.

"Inside joke," I said, waving it off. *You're hilarious, Ahbi.*

She snorted, but kept quiet after that.

"Our order has always been autonomous," Bakari said, becoming serious again. "No Ruler has ever dictated terms. My order was specifically designed to watch over the safety of Demonicon—something that at times went against the rule of some on First Seat."

"Understandable," I said. It made a great deal of sense to me. Though I wondered what they'd all been doing the last four years while I stumbled and crashed my way through my initial attempts to rule. "You could have let me know a little earlier. Some help would have been nice."

Bakari shrugged. "We needed to see what kind of Ruler you would become," he said.

"And?" I planted my hands on my hips, staring at him through lidded eyes, just daring him to say the wrong thing while I worried he might tell me what I was afraid to hear.

"And," he said, a real smile on his face, "though we thought initially we would be forced to take steps to remove you, you have shown remarkable advances in the face of true adversity." He winked, so out of character for him I blinked in surprise. "We'll keep you."

"Nice of you," I said, though I did admit in the quiet of my own mind it was a relief to know they didn't plan to murder me in my sleep. "When is the meeting?"

"Whenever you are ready," Bakari said, all cold business again. "We understand the threat to your life has become dire and would take steps to protect you."

I thought of Zinnia and her people and made a startled connection. "You sent her, didn't you?"

Bakari didn't respond, though the fact I only referred to my father's ex-fiancé as "her" was rather telling. He knew exactly who I was talking about.

Ahbi's troubled mind stirred. *I'm beginning to think I was fooling myself*, she sent. *From all the things I've learned since you and your sister crashed Demonicon's party, I'm realizing I knew far less than I thought I did.*

Don't feel bad, I sent. *I know I'm in the dark.*

Sometimes that's more helpful, Ahbi sent, soft and pensive before falling silent again.

"Ruler." Sequoia stepped forward, Sassafras in her arms, Jabut towering over me from behind so his shadow cast darkness on Bakari. "We can't let you go alone."

"Absolutely not." Sass's tail hit his sister's arm so hard I heard the thud. His flat gaze shifted to the assassin, ears straight back, whiskers bristling. "Don't even think about it."

Bakari bowed to the demon cat. "I wouldn't dream of it," he said. "You have all proven yourselves valuable and trustworthy. I am permitted to bring two others with Ruler."

I turned to my friends as all three opened their mouths, shaking my head with one hand raised to stop their arguments as to why they should accompany me. The moment I did, a vast gust of air pushed against me as the shields around the balcony parted. Mabel leaped through. I caught the very last of her transformation from flying drach to humanoid as she landed with cat-like agility on the stone floor, her gray robe and floor-length black hair settling around her. Her diamond eyes flashed in the light, a small smile lifting her lips.

"Ruler," she said. "I have come to aid you, if I can."

So much relief poured over me at the sight of her, I laughed and clapped my hands like a little girl before I could stop myself. I pulled back my emotions, but refused to squash them completely. Let Bakari judge me if he wanted. But I wouldn't school myself against how I felt for any of them any longer.

"Lovely to have you," I beamed at the drach. "And decision made."

Mabel glided forward, chin tilting as she approached. "Decision?"

I turned back to Bakari. "Sassafras," I said. "And Mabel."

The brief look of worry crossing the assassin's face gave me great satisfaction.

I squeezed my hands together to keep from itching at the edge of the blindfold hiding my eyes from the world around me. Ahbi stewed in anger, pacing inside my head so quickly I felt dizzy behind the dark cloth.

Grandmother, I sent. *Please, you're making me nauseated.*

She stopped her spinning, settling, though her indignant fury didn't ease.

Imagine, she sent, spit actually, with real venom. *This is ridiculous. A blindfold of all stupid, pathetic, untrusting—*

Grandmother. I released my hands long enough to press them to my temples, a throbbing headache starting up now that she'd stopped making my stomach flip. *Seriously, you're killing me, here.*

Magic swirled, soothed my aching mind. I dropped my hands again, fingers brushing over the soft fabric wound around my eyes as Ahbi sighed.

Sorry, she sent before pausing a moment. *I seem to be apologizing to you a great deal, lately.*

What a novelty, I sent, though with humor to take the sarcastic edge away. *It's fine. We're both frustrated. But at least we're here.* At least, I assumed we were "here", as in the order's territory. Bakari had immediately guided me to the balcony window and removed the illusion of invisibility from around the transport he'd brought. It was far too small for Mabel to join us, though Sassafras eagerly leaped into my lap.

It was hard to wave goodbye to the anxious Pagomaris, nearly frantic Jabut, and hesitant Sequoia, their faces disappearing behind the blindfold before Bakari took to the air. I heard him murmur with Mabel, the rush of air and the flap of her wings and could only assume she somehow convinced him to allow her to join us with her sight unhindered.

The transport rocked gently as he settled and I felt the zinging pop of the shields snapping into place. Sassafras sat, heavy and hot, in my lap, kneading my knee gently in comfort, purring under his breath. I didn't know if it was meant to calm me or himself, but I took advantage of his closeness to gently stroke his fur over and over.

This is perfect. Ahbi's chortle of glee made me grin.

How so? My body tilted as the transport banked to the right.

You might be blindfolded, she sent, *but my magic can still have a look around.* She reached out, only to flinch back and start grumbling.

You were saying? I suppose I should have warned her I'd already tried to explore the world around me with my power, in fact that I did so the instant the blindfold settled on my eyes, with about as much luck.

You could have said, she groused.

I could have, I sent. *But I thought you were paying attention.* My fingers slid over the small hood Sassafras wore, testing the edge to ensure it wasn't too tight.

I'm fine, he sent. *But the fabric seems to have some kind of blocking magic built in.*

It does, I sent. *Empty magic.*

Sorcery. Ahbi grunted. *Damn it.*

Mabel is free out there, I sent.

I am here, Ruler, the drach's mind touched mine. *I won't let anything happen to you.* She paused a moment. *Is it typical of your people to gather in large numbers?*

Why do you ask? I shifted in my seat, hands reaching for my blindfold again.

A group of demons has assemble at the base of the Seat, Mabel sent. *They seemed peaceful enough, but I'm unaware of their purpose.*

Your grandfather probably ordered some kind of assembly, Ahbi hissed. *He's making his move while we're trapped behind magicked fabric, going who knows where at the whim of a sect so untrusting it's taken this long for them to allow a Ruler to visit.*

"Bakari." I resisted the urge to kick the seat ahead of me with one heavy platform boot, just from sheer spite. "What's happening?"

"Our people are watching," he said. "I believe Ahbi is correct, however." Eavesdropping made me furious. "Henemordonin continues to pull the strings of power in every effort to oust you."

"Will you let that happen?" It would be nice to have his order on my side.

"Perhaps you should ask, Ruler," he said in his cold voice as we banked to the right, "if you will let it happen. Because, if so, you aren't the leader we thought you were."

Asshat, Ahbi grumbled. *Isn't he a piece of work?*

I will not, Mabel sent, warming the chill mood in the transport. *For now, I will monitor this for you. But I believe speaking with Bakari's people is important, Meira. You can do nothing about your grandfather's betrayals until you have found a way to stabilize Demonicon.*

I shivered and sat back, trying to trust she knew what she was talking about.

It was hard to tell how much time passed and, no matter how sweetly I asked questions or made comments, Bakari remained silent so I finally gave up. It was perhaps a half hour later I felt the transport slow and settle. Before I could speak up, the shields collapsed in a rush of dying power and the hull rocked gently. I reached out with both hands for Bakari, only to find the front seat empty. I barely had time to lift Sass into my arms before a strong grip guided me up and out of the small hull and onto the hard stone floor.

The air was cool, damp, smelling faintly of the earth. Now that the shields were down, I swallowed and felt my ears pop, no longer protected from the change of altitude.

We're underground, Ahbi sent.

Clearly, Sassafras snapped.

A rush of air buffeted me, the rustle of fabric close by as a gentle, if giant, hand settled on my right shoulder.

"I am here, Ruler," Mabel's deep voice rumbled over my head. "I will guide her from here."

The hand on my arm disappeared, the drach's grip tightening slightly on my shoulder as it did.

"Very well," Bakari's voice said. "This way."

I stumbled my first step, Sassafras hissing at me to be careful as my arms reflexively grasped him tighter.

"Sorry," I muttered as Mabel's hands held me upright.

"The floor is smooth and uninterrupted by obstacles," Mabel said. "Trust me to guide you. I will not let you fall."

I relaxed under her hands and nodded.

"Lead the way," I said.

"The elders are waiting." Bakari's voice echoed. I had the impression of a vast, empty space, the faint sound of water dripping somewhere to my right. I turned my head toward it as I strode with confidence born of trust in Mabel following the assassin. We walked for at least twenty paces before Mabel's hand slowed me gently, turning me to the left. The feeling of a massive void vanished, the air more closed.

"Stairs," Mabel said, giving me the gentlest push. "There is the first. They go upward for some distance."

The first one was a bit of a trick, but I quickly fell into the rhythm and was surprised when Mabel slowed me again.

"Last one," she said. "Turning right."

I felt her shift behind me, one boot impacting what felt like a threshold, the feeling of the air being broken telling me I'd walked through a doorway. A breeze brushed over my cheek, a touch of silken hair. Mabel must have been forced to duck to make her way through.

She guided me forward and stopped me at last.

"Sit," she said, both hands turning me by my shoulders and pressing down softly until I sank onto a hard, cold surface. "We have arrived, I believe." She shifted behind me, still there, the heat of her body close at my back. Sassafras wriggled out of my grip, settling into my lap where he shook his head, the fabric of his hood brushing over my hands.

"Enough already," he growled. "I want this thing off."

"Patience." Bakari's voice retreated.

He's gone, Mabel sent instead of speaking.

Where are we? I could only guess at the reason she remained unfettered.

She's drach, Ahbi sent. *As if anyone could stop her if they wanted to.*

Mabel's voice rumbled in my mind, the hugeness of it full of humor. *Indeed*, she sent. *I assured him I would not confess his secrets.* She seemed immensely amused by the whole thing. *What interesting creatures you demons are.*

Thank you, I sent to her, trying to find the funny in it, too.

Time passed, enough for my grandmother to lose her temper. And, I admit, even though I admonished her to wait it out, by the time she eased my headache, I was ready to take the damned blindfold off myself and have done with it.

They come, Mabel sent to the sound of rustling straight ahead of me. I perked, Sass shifting in my lap while Ahbi fell silent and waited.

Bakari approaches, Mabel sent.

The blindfold came off in a quick jerk, though I like to think he didn't intend to snap my head forward the way he did. Sassafras snarled at him as his hood slid free, even as I blinked into the dim light of the room, gaze focusing on the three old demons sitting in tall-backed chairs only a few feet ahead of me.

"Senne Hathenemeira," the one in the middle, a wizened old demon female said in a voice like sharpened crystal. "Welcome to the home of the Order of Daeva."

CHAPTER FOURTEEN

I felt Ahbi stir but cut her off before her "helpful suggestions" could start in a steady stream of confusing me.

"Thank you," I said with as much humble appreciation as I could muster.

Ahbi's mind snapped against mine. *What are you doing?* Her anger popped and crackled. *You are RULER. Do not give them leeway.*

Grandmother. I firmly pushed her back. *I'm handling this. Now hush.*

She stomped her mental foot before turning her back on me.

The lead demon watched with a blank expression, though as I took control, she nodded.

"You are the first of your kind to be admitted here," the demon leader said. "We take a great risk in bringing you among us."

"I hope you know I would never put your order at risk," I said.

"Not on purpose." She shook her head. "But there are those who hunt you now, Ruler of Demonicon. And they have means to find you wherever you go."

That's not what we wanted to hear, Sassafras sent.

Demon cat, the woman's voice spoke in my head, dry and crisp, *you will voice your words aloud at this time.*

He bowed his head to her, mane still ruffled from his time under the hood. "I will," he said. "But because I choose to."

"Gently," I murmured to him. "We're not enemies, here."

Sass settled as the woman nodded.

"You show great maturity of spirit for one so exceedingly young," she said. "I am Raethnn, and I speak for the Daeva." She didn't try to introduce the two older male demons, one on either side of her, so I didn't push the matter. Raethnn's long-fingered, skeletal hands rose, her elbows on her arm rests, long nails clacking as she wound her fingers together before her. "We have never needed to speak directly to one such as you. This is the first time in the history of Demonicon we are unable to protect what we have been charged with, and only for that reason do we call on you for an alliance."

"I understand," I said. "May I ask—how much do

you know of sorcery?"

She laughed, a dusty sound, her ice-white hair sparkling in the low light as she nodded. "Much more than you," she said. "We have been observing you, to see what you might accomplish on your own. You have uncovered much more than we ever expected, though I suppose that is our failing. You are, after all, not born of Demonicon, nor are you a full demon." I did my best not to bristle against the statement. I'd heard it before, hated the "half breed" label I'd caught whispered among the court. It was easy to let it pass, because Raethnn didn't say it with derision—just as a statement of fact. "As it turns out, it may have been the best thing to happen to the First Seat since its inception. At least, we are hopeful of your development from this point on."

Even I admit that's high praise, Ahbi sent.

"I'm doing my best," I said. "But help is always welcome."

Raethnn nodded. "And that is the reason we have finally broken our silence and welcomed you here. You are willing to listen."

Even Ahbi perked, turning back around. *I would have listened*, she sent.

Raethnn laughed with enthusiasm, teeth bright against her age-darkened skin. "Ahbi Sanghamitra," she said, "you, of all Rulers, would not. But we respected you and trusted you to do what you needed."

My grandmother settled, anger gone. *Fair enough*, she sent.

Raethnn settled, hands falling to her lap as her two counterparts grinned, though neither appeared to be as amused as she. "In order to understand what we face, a history lesson is in order. Though what we are about to tell you has never before left the halls of our order." The door behind them opened, a door I only then noticed, and Zinnia slipped through. I had already guessed she was part of the Daeva, though seeing her there still gave me a zip of surprise.

"A question, first." I pointed at the gorgeous young demon who came to stand behind Raethnn. "What was Zinnia's purpose?" I caught myself frowning and released my irritation as I worked the details out. "And how did she hide her intent from me?" I was so sure I understood her motives, her vapid emptiness clearly a ploy to put me at ease.

Zinnia spoke before Raethnn could. "May I?"

The old demon nodded. "Proceed, great-granddaughter."

It was obvious Raethnn addressed Zinnia that way on purpose, wanting me to know who she was. I was fine with the reveal, as unsubtle as it was, but not so much with the understanding I'd been played by the people around me with such ease.

"I am Bakari's sister," she said with a smile, gesturing

to the silent demon standing out of the way on my right. He was barely visible in the dim glow overhead, as though a part of the stone room instead of a living, breathing demon. "Our jobs were diverse, but had the same goal. To watch over the Seat."

The realization she was Ram's aunt wasn't lost on me. "You used sorcery to disguise your purpose." It made sense, now. I felt the empty coldness of the black under the quiet of the shielding in the room. How had I missed it?

But Zinnia shook her head. "I didn't have to," she said, her voice gentle. "My intent was always pure."

Ahbi tsked, but stayed quiet.

"I was going to marry your father," Zinnia said, "to protect Demonicon."

"From what?" I glanced down from Zinnia to Raethnn who watched me with careful eyes.

"From Haralthazar," Zinnia said, her tone still warm and kind. "When we realized what he was trying to do, we had to act. It was my job to guide him. But he stepped down before we could complete the mating and you were put on the throne." She sighed and slumped. "I failed. And I was at a loss how to help you, considering you hated me for what I was about to do with your beloved father."

That much was very true. My loyalty to my parents was far stronger than my pity for her. Now that Mom and

Dad were together for the rest of their lives, my father's longevity stunted by the destruction of his effigy, I could afford to be more forgiving.

"Demons are not meant to rule by committee," Raethnn said. "It is not our nature to do so. The only thing we understand as a race is power. This isn't some delusion or old way of thinking." She jabbed a thin finger at me. "We allowed this demonocracy to develop, to see if perhaps we were wrong. But it is clear only corruption can come from such a method, thanks to the nature of our race."

"Maybe," I said. "Though there are parts of it that could work with the right leadership."

And with your grandfather dead, Ahbi sent.

"While we have evolved past our primitive nature," Raethnn said, "we are, in essence, creatures of fire. And though we could move past our ways eventually, en masse our race suffers from too much power hunger for it to succeed."

I agree, Ahbi sent.

Sadly, so did I.

"Only the unification and enforcement of law has kept us from devolving back into our feudal state," Zinnia said. "We had hoped perhaps the influence of your witch blood might make it more likely to succeed. But we have watched you struggle to take control to no avail."

Shame burned bright in my heart. "It's been difficult," I said while Ahbi bristled.

She's done her best, my grandmother sent.

"It would appear the challenges of the Planeless and the troubling Node attacks have brought out your ability to act," Raethnn said. "Which is why you are here. It is our hope you can finally reach your potential and lead the rest of Demonicon while we do what we do best."

"Which is?" I felt Sassafras stir under my hands as he growled softly.

"Hunt those who threaten our people," Raethnn said, all demanity gone from her voice, now as statuesque as Bakari. "And kill them."

I'm all for that, Ahbi sent.

"If you could have done so," Sassafras spoke up suddenly, "you would have by now."

Raethnn's eyes flashed a frown pulling at her lips. But she wasn't angry at the demon cat. "You speak absolute truth, Sassafras," she said. "We have carried out our sacred duty since the formation of Demonicon. Never before have we failed." Her hands rose and fell on the armrests of her chair with a solid thump despite her thin frame. "Never. Until now."

"Thus your desire to work with me." Finally. I nodded, glancing sideways at Bakari. "Tell me why you've been watching my grandfather."

"Because we do not trust him," Raethnn said with a

128

hiss of venom. "We have never trusted him. Nor should you."

I figured that out centuries ago, Ahbi sent.

"He's a pain in my ass," I said. "But he would never put the safety of Demonicon at risk."

"It is for that reason and that reason only," Bakari spoke up, "he is still alive."

"But his foolish attempts to wrest power from you, his focus on this ridiculous demonocracy," Raethnn's nose wrinkled as she spoke, "has put Demonicon at greater risk than he knows. He is so focused on power hunger, he can't see the larger danger."

"The Planeless." I shuddered, Sass looking up at me with glowing eyes. "They're responsible for the loss of planes in the Node, aren't they?"

"They are." Raethnn shifted in her seat, gesturing behind me. I turned, glancing past Mabel, to see Pagomaris approaching. I stared in shock, partly because she was here, but more so because she no longer carried herself like a servant. Back straight, face grim, my aide—a member of this order, I now understood—came to stand beside me, nodding to her leader.

Pagomaris nodded to me without a hint of remorse as Ahbi gasped and swore. "The Planeless are using sorcery," she said. "As we do. Ours was left uncapped when the first Ruler created Demonicon. All others of the demon race had theirs blocked off."

"And with good reason," Zinnia said. "The Node was created using sorcery."

The Node was what? Ahbi gasped.

"The balance of the Node's hold over all planes is a delicate one," Raethnn said. "But it's not as delicate as most demons are led to believe. Your sister and her fight with the one known as Ameline could not have broken the seals of the Node unless they had both resorted to using only sorcery." I gaped at her while my brain turned in spinning circles. "Demons are not permitted to use their sorcery, for fear they will shatter the Node apart." I felt Mabel shift behind me, breaking my stunned silence.

"All demons have sorcery." I shuddered. "This is a giant secret."

"One that has remained hidden for as long as Demonicon existed," Raethnn said. "Only our order was permitted the use of sorcery, because we know how do to so without damaging the Node." Her face twisted, a hint of distress finally showing. "Have you wondered why demons are not permitted to strip each other of their power, Meira?" I didn't complain at her use of my common name, so absorbed was I in this revelation. Sassafras perked as the old assassin continued. "It is not the stripping of magic that concerns us. It is the worry once the fire elemental power is gone, the stripped demon's sorcery will wake and the truth will come out."

"That is why when a demon is stripped," Zinnia said,

"they are usually killed immediately."

"I wasn't." Sassafras's voice trembled. "My father kept my body."

"He did," Raethnn said. "It was unfortunate we were forced to sabotage it to keep you from returning to it, Sassafras."

They. Did. Not.

He shuddered in my arms. "I understand," he whispered.

"I don't." I glared, anger finally tripped. "What about other demons who have been stripped but remain alive and well?" I dug my fingers into my sad cat's fur. "Raneesh, for example." The young demon Sassafras stripped, the very reason he was in the body of a cat and had been banished by Ahbi to my home plane so many years ago, remained in the care of his parents.

"A simple visit," Raethnn said, "and such demons are not a problem any longer. Their blocks are reinforced regularly."

"Be angry with us if you must," Pagomaris said, "but, Meira, you must understand. The safety of our entire world is at stake."

I shook my head, but not in denial. So many clues and puzzle pieces were falling together at once I could barely process them. "The monster inside us," I said. "The one that rises when we strip demons. That's sorcery, isn't it?" I met Raethnn's eyes.

She nodded. "Very good, Meira," she said. "It is the second reason why such things are usually illegal or, if necessary, done in controlled circumstances. One demon, set loose with their sorcery fed by the power of two souls, could destroy everything." She shifted in her seat, leaning forward. "Now you understand the reason for our order, and why we remain apart. We must watch and guard for such instances. Should the sorcerous seals between planes be fed by errant power, the planes will come apart again."

I shuddered at the thought of Syd and Ameline's fight inside the Node and how close they came to doing what Syd tried to prevent.

"Someone is using sorcery," Raethnn said, "to surgically remove planes from the Node, one at a time." Her hands twisted together in a visible sign of stress. "And we have no idea how."

"Or why," Zinnia said. "But we do know who."

"Xeoniteridone," I said.

Raethnn sat back again while her two counterparts looked uncomfortable. "He came to us several years ago," she said. "Xeoniteridone arrived out of nowhere, claiming to have control of his sorcery. We studied him, though when he began to share his plans for his little cult, we tried to have him killed." She grimaced. "He escaped as easily as if we were simple guards and he a ghost." Her sharp eyes locked me in place as she went on. "But one thing we know for certain—he came, not from the planes of Demonicon, but from your birth world, Meira." She exhaled sharply as my stomach cramped at the news. "And if we can't find a way to stop him, he will destroy us all."

CHAPTER FIFTEEN

If you've known about him and the Planeless, Ahbi's sharp anger cut through my spinning mind, *why did you not act well before now?*

"We've tried," Bakari said. "We've been trying for over a year."

I'd never felt so shaken and vulnerable as I did sitting there, with the understanding even those who thought themselves all-powerful had failed. Maybe I should have felt better about myself and my own disasters, but I didn't.

Their inability just made things worse. Sure, I was off the hook in a lot of ways. If the Daeva couldn't handle the Planeless, there was no way I could be expected to. And yet, the way they looked at me, that was exactly their expectation.

"So he's like me, then?" I resisted the words even as I

spoke them. Xeoniteridone was nothing like me. "Half witch, half demon?"

"We believe so," Raethnn said. "At least, that was what he told us."

"Meira, he's a sorcerer," Sassafras said. "It's much more likely one of his parents was from that magical race and not a witch."

It made perfect sense, almost symmetrical and terribly beautiful. "What's your current plan to take him out?"

"Every one of our order we send after Xeoniteridone turns," Raethnn said, eyes sparking amber fire. "Our plans have all failed. You are our next phase in counter-attack, Meira." She tapped her long, thick nails on the arms of her chair. "It is my fault. We should have come to you sooner. And I failed Rameranselot by keeping him in the dark about the Planeless." Bakari twitched, face darkening. "The boy didn't know we were tracing the cult and didn't contact us about his plans to investigate. Had he, we would never have allowed him to put himself at risk."

"My failing, not yours, Raethnn," Bakari said. "I insisted on keeping the truth from my son to protect him."

"And, in doing so," Raethnn's voice cracked whip-like across the room, "we have lost him."

It was easy to be angry, to allow my temper to build and burn despite my need to remain calm with my new allies. So many mistakes, so much pride, and all too many lies had led us to this place and the imminent destruction of Demonicon. But screaming and yelling at Raethnn and her fellow elders would get me nowhere. I could see in the tightness around her eyes, hear in the rapid patter of her rock-hard nails on the armrests of her chair just how much she wished things had gone differently, too.

I drew a deep breath and let it out, forcing myself to return to rational thinking.

"You had enough of your kind watching over me," I said. And though I was determined to keep my temper in check, I was unable to wash the stiff disapproval from my voice. "You could have warned me."

"Ruler always has multiple watchers from the order," she said with a wave of one hand. "And we were certain you would be of no assistance."

That bit you in the ass, didn't it? Ahbi sighed. *Now what?*

Raethnn shrugged, though it was an angry gesture. "We must work together," she said. "And think outside our norm. Again, this is why you are here." Her gaze lifted over my shoulder. "And why we allowed the drach to join us, unfettered."

Mabel's huge body shifted behind me. "We have known of your task since you were created," she said. "But, though we have chosen Demonicon as our home for part of the time, we have lost track of the dealings of your order and allowed you to carry on without assistance." Her deep voice filled the room with so much sound my ears ached. "There are more issues requiring our attention beyond the fate of Demonicon at this time, but I have been instructed by," she sang a few notes I recognized as Max's drach name, "to offer what aid I am able to ensure disaster does not occur." She set one hand on my shoulder. "Even we drach have no idea what will happen if Demonicon falls. Since the separating planes seem to be stable and the Universe yet stands," the irony in her voice was so subtle I'm sure I was the only one to pick it up, "we can postulate the dissolution will have no effect."

"But you're guessing," Raethnn said, eyes narrow. "We could use more drach to assist us."

I bristled immediately, knowing what a mess they faced, what my sister faced, out there in the veil. But Mabel had it covered.

"Indeed," Mabel said, as calm and dry as ever. "But might I remind you, Daeva leader, the Universe does not revolve around Demonicon." She allowed that to sink in a moment before going on. "The veil itself is in danger. One plane—or a collection of such—falling into its original state does not constitute as large a threat as the very shield between us and the other dark Universe falling completely."

Raethnn nodded, mouth curving downward in frustration.

"We are very grateful to have you." I half-turned and reached for Mabel's hand, squeezing her fingers. She returned my grip softly before releasing me.

"I must warn you," she said, "even I cannot seem to counter the power of the Planeless, and am baffled as to the reason. But I can tell you, I have every faith in Ruler."

That was a shock and a compliment so massive, I wasn't sure I deserved it. But when I turned back, Raethnn was nodding in agreement.

"What of the nectar they use to suppress the power of their converts?" I clutched at Sassafras who purred without sound, his body's vibration helping me calm.

"We are aware," the old demon said. "But are embarrassed to admit, we didn't make the connection until it was far too late."

"And Theridialis?" Sassafras's ears drooped. "What of my father's fate?"

"We don't know," Raethnn said with a tone of real regret. "We can only assume he has been taken by the Planeless for their own purposes."

Arrogant, Ahbi sent. *You've been in power for centuries, assigned as the guardians of Demonicon, working without barriers or limits and out of the oversight of the Seat. And this is what you've become.* She snarled so loudly Sassafras jumped in my lap. *You've failed us all, Raethnn, you and the Daeva. So complacent in your smug superiority you've allowed a single intruder to undo the most complex magical construct ever successfully completed. And now, thanks to you and your imperious need to cling to the old ways and your refusal to admit you need help, you've opened the doorway to Demonicon coming under attack that will surely put an end to millennia of evolution.*

I cleared my throat as Raethnn and her fellow elders shifted in their chairs, their only visible sign they'd heard Ahbi's rant. I was personally grateful my grandmother spoke what I'd been thinking all along. At least this way I could play good cop to her very bad, very angry one. "Regardless of the past," I said, "we have to focus on the future. No more blame or guilt. That can all come later, once we've figured out how to heal our world."

The Deava trio nodded.

Traitor, Ahbi sent.

Not at all, Mabel sent to both of us. *You've said your piece, Ahbi Sanghamitra, and your message was received. They are already deep in their own despair. I can feel it. More attacks will only worsen our situation. Meira, please proceed.*

Ahbi grumbled but fell quiet as I silently thanked the drach for her voice of reason.

"But we doubt very much the Planeless would have killed Theridialis," Zinnia spoke up, kind eyes on Sassafras as she dragged us back to the topic at hand. "If they wanted him dead, they would simply have ended his life, not kidnapped him." She dropped her hands to her sides, hands she must have only then noticed she was wringing slightly. "I can only suppose he was close to a cure to the nectar. It's possible they lured him to his lab in order to make him easier to kidnap and less likely for you, Ruler, to discover until it was too late." Her sad eyes fell on Sassafras again. "In fact, it's likely your father was successful in his tests. It's the only explanation for his capture." She glanced sideways at her leaders. "Which worries me, not for his safety, but for ours. Such a talented scientist would be valuable to Xeoniteridone. And could mean a newer, more powerful, strain of the nectar might soon be available."

"Father would never help them," Sassafras spit, fur bristling.

"He would if he were under their spell," Zinnia said, voice soft and careful.

"Theridialis fought them," I said. "If he has, as you said, come up with an antidote, it's likely he tested it on himself." I'd seen him do so many times with other potions, happily and, to my sharp concern, gleefully, dosing himself with things I was sure even he wasn't certain he could control. "Which means he'll be immune to the nectar, if nothing else."

"Even more reason for Xeoniteridone to keep him alive," Zinnia said. "If there is an antidote, the cult leader will require Theridialis to either counter his own treatment or create a new, unstoppable nectar."

All speculation. It was quite possible Theridialis was dead, dumped somewhere, his power drained from him, and that he'd never achieved an antidote at all. But I needed to feel optimistic, to keep myself going. And everything Zinnia said was exactly what I thought. Though hearing someone else say Theridialis's value to the Planeless was enough to keep him alive, as I suspected, made me feel much better. It was a small comfort, but Sassafras's ears twitched back to normal. "Agreed," he said.

"As far as we can tell," Raethnn said, "Xeoniteridone is using the nectar to silence the fire elemental power of the demons who follow him. Some he is now triggering, allowing their sorcery to awaken. Though he is smart enough, it seems to control them still. We believe the disappearance of the planes from the Node is not so much a byproduct of their freedom, but a surgical strike against the core of power itself."

"To what end?" It made no sense. Why shrink his available power source?

"We have, as yet, to uncover that truth." Raethnn sighed again, shrinking in on herself a moment until, instead of a vital and powerful—if older—demon, she looked tired and very much every year of her age. "But we must understand him, and soon, if we are to stop him."

"I'm going to need help," I said. "And open communication." I glanced at Bakari, then Zinnia. "I'll take all three of these, if that works for you?" Pagomaris twitched beside me.

Raethnn nodded. "As you wish."

I stood, stepping forward. "And, if you don't mind," I said, "though at this point, we don't have a choice, I want to bring one more person in on this." I had to ask her. She was the only one I knew of who had the power—aside from Mabel and her kind—with access to sorcery and the knowledge to use it.

Raethnn hesitated. "You speak of your sister." She sounded like she didn't approve.

"Like it or not," I said, "approve of her or not, we're going to need Syd."

I pulled free the blindfold Raethnn insisted I wear on the way back and found myself standing in my quarters, Sequoia and Jabut anxiously watching me. Bakari didn't vanish as I expected him to, and I could tell by the worried look on my friend's faces, the appearance of Zinnia and Pagomaris in combination had thrown them for as big a loop as it had me.

Sassafras I deposited on a chair with a soft stroke to his mussed fur, the hood puddling on the floor below his perch. I kicked it away, the hateful thing as distasteful to me as the blindfold I'd worn. Bakari retrieved both without a word, tucking the pieces of cloth into his clothing as I turned to face my friends.

"Ruler." Sequoia's concern seemed excessive,

considering we were back, safe and sound. "We have a situation developing."

I looked back and forth between the two siblings while Mabel frowned.

"The gathering below the Seat has grown to a large number," the drach said. I scowled at the balcony, cursing my grandfather and his power grab. He really had terrible timing.

"It will have to wait," I said. Before either Sequoia or Jabut could interrupt, I grimly told them about our new alliance with the Daeva.

Both were suitably shocked when they discovered the truth of sorcery, though from the black look on Bakari's face, I was speaking out of turn, as far as he was concerned. I glared at him.

"You want my help?" I poked him in the chest with one stiff finger, hard enough to make him retreat. "You trust the people I trust."

"Because you know them so well," he said, gaze lifting to fall on someone behind me. I spun and fixed my anger on Pagomaris. She hadn't retreated to her aide act, at least, though she did look rather contrite.

"I trust her," I said, even as my temper bit me deep. "Daeva or not, a liar or not," Pagomaris twitched at my words, "she has stood by both my grandmother and myself with courage and faithfulness." I jabbed Bakari again. "I might not have known she was one of you, but I know her." I pointed at my aide. "I know her heart." Why did I suddenly think of Ram? I didn't have time for the tiny seed of hope that woke in my chest, the whisper of the his heart. I knew him, too, didn't I?

Bakari nodded. "Very well," he said. "We must proceed with haste."

"I fear your plan to utilize your sister is flawed, Ruler." I turned to Mabel who looked troubled, her diamond eyes dim.

"The veil." I knew Syd had more than enough of her own trouble on her hands, what with the damage Gabriel had done when he opened the Gateway to the other Universe. But the drach were on it, weren't they? I needed Syd.

"It is so," Mabel said. "My people find themselves in a battle not only against the virus-like destruction to parts of the veil between Universes, they are also struggling to return the few creatures who have passed over to our realm who have no right or place here."

I didn't ask her what kind of creatures the drach—the first race of our Universe—might not be able to just eliminate with their power. I didn't want to know.

"Sydlynn is of great assistance," Mabel said. "The maji continue to ignore our requests for aid. Having her, at least, to augment our abilities has been of large benefit. And yet, if Demonicon falls, I know she will blame herself for its passing."

Syd would. The rejection of the second race—the maji—would just make her more determined to fix things herself. And guilt was second nature to her. But not any more than I.

"I'll try to reach her anyway," I said. "But if we're on our own, we are." There had to be a way to stop the Planeless. And I would not stop until I found it.

I turned from the watching demons and led Mabel aside. *Can you help me find her?*

I can, the drach sent. Her hand enfolded mine, the hot flesh making my palm sweat. Her vast, infinite mind opened, though I felt her shielding me from the the impact of her enormous presence. Still, by the time I felt her reach into the veil, it wasn't just my hand that was sweating.

Meems. Syd's mental voice was as strong as I was used to, though she sounded impatient and distracted. I caught a tiny glimpse of the back of Max's drach head and neck, felt her perched on his back while the air before her in the dark of the veil crackled with what looked like static. *Are you okay?*

I am, I sent. *But I have a lot to tell you.* My heart pounded as the image snapped shut, just before a swarm of what looked like giant wasps swooped into Syd's view.

Kind of busy, she sent in a tight jab.

Be safe, I sent and let her go. I felt her reach for me again, but retreated, releasing Mabel's hand with a sigh.

"Thank you," I said. "She's right. I'm going to have to do this myself."

"Not alone," Mabel said, bowing her head to me.

"Your people need you." I stepped back from her, hating to let her go, but knowing what the drach were doing was more important. Demonicon was one plane—well, it was for now—while the threat to the veil was immense.

"My people do not," Mabel said. "I informed Max before I left I would not return until Demonicon was stable and I intend to fulfill that promise."

I could have hugged her, but resisted the urge. "Thank you."

When I turned back to the others, the disappointed looks on their faces told me they already guessed Syd wasn't coming to the rescue.

"No need to be so glum," I said, forcing a measure of cheer. "Mabel's staying."

That fact seemed to reassure them, though Bakari continued to scowl.

"Ruler." Jabut bowed abruptly. "My investigation of the Planeless infiltration turned up nothing. Forgive me."

I crossed to him and patted his arm, pacing on by as my mind tried to process I was in charge. No Syd rushing in to save me. And though Mabel was much stronger, older and more experienced—not to mention she was a dragon, for goodness sakes, and practically

146

indestructible—she seemed quite willing to wait and accept my lead.

"Above all else," Zinnia said, "we must find a way to protect you from them."

I turned back, stopped my pacing. "I can't believe I'm going to say this," I said, shaking my head while Ahbi hissed at me, "but I need to tell Henemordonin what's happening."

"Forgive my bluntness," Sassafras said with enough sarcasm I knew he meant nothing of the sort, "but you've tried that before, haven't you?"

"He's Second Seat," I grated through my aching jaw as my teeth clenched and unclenched against the idea. "He has to listen this time. Demonicon is in terrible danger."

Sequoia shook her head, distress on her doll-like face. "Whether you want to or not," she said, "I'm afraid it's quite impossible at the moment."

"Why is that?" I felt my stomach clench against the feeling of "what now?" as she spoke.

"I'm sorry," she wrung her hands, "in all the excitement, I failed to tell you." She shivered. "Henemordonin is gone."

"What?"

What?

Ahbi and I said it together in a rush of shock.

Jabut stepped to his sister's side as Sassafras hissed at

no one in particular. "It's true," he said, normally booming voice soft. "No one knows where he's gone."

I instantly reached for my grandfather, chasing out toward the familiar nastiness of his mind, the pressure of his magic, the feeling of him simple enough for me to focus on, it was so well known to me.

And came up empty.

Curse all that is unholy, Ahbi sent. *Did they kidnap him, too?*

"Either the Planeless took him," Sequoia barely spoke above a whisper, "or…"

"Or he's done something incredibly stupid," I said. "Like go after them himself."

No one moved or spoke for a long moment. Part of me hoped he was gone, a terrible and bitter part. Maybe this would mean the end of him.

Not so terrible, Ahbi sent.

Grandmother. I had no right to chide her.

Before I could fully comprehend what his absence meant or make a plan around my newfound return to singular rule, the door to my chamber was loudly pounded upon before Elph burst through. The handsome young demon was so distressed, I strode immediately to his side and led him deeper into the room. He grasped at my hands, looking around at my watching friends with wild eyes.

"Ruler," he said. "You must come quickly."

Oh, for the sake of the Node, what now? Ahbi's groan hid her fear only about as well as my sharp intake of breath.

"What's wrong?" Exactly what I needed at this moment, more strife.

He swallowed hard, regaining some control. "The populace of Ostrogotho has noticed something is wrong with the sky," he said. "That suns and moons have gone missing. And they've gathered in the Parade demanding answers."

Sequoia meeped, Jabut grunting at the same time.

"We tried to tell you," the tiny demon said.

I spun on them, heart pounding. "I thought Henemordonin called an assembly." Mabel mentioned it when we were leaving to talk to the Daeva. Why the big deal?

"Not to my knowledge," Jabut said. "Though, I admit, I'm not in his circles. But he's been missing since last night."

Mabel strode to the balcony. "The crowd does, indeed, seem more feisty than they were earlier. As though they are waiting for someone with increasing impatience."

"How many?" Sassafras hopped down from his seat and went to the balcony. I rushed after him, the rest of my friends behind me while Elph continued to hold my hand. I leaned over the edge, Sequoia lifting her furry brother to see, and looked down at the vast—if tiny from this distance—parade space at the base of the mountain.

It was packed with writhing, ant-like movement, the shining stone blacked out by the teeming gathering.

"All of them," Elph whispered.

Chapter Sixteen

The tightly-packed guards surrounded me, their magic forcing the crowd aside, creating a space for me to mount the platform at the base of the mountain. The court followed me with more fear than eagerness, their desire to remain behind while I dealt with things so palpable when I stormed into the throne room just a few minutes earlier, I smelled their fear in the air.

"The court goes as a group," I snapped, power crackling and offering no recourse. "Unless there's a damned stupid law against it. And you'd better show me proof if there is one."

No one could and I saw just how much that distressed them. Maybe I should have let them remain behind. As we descended in bunches from the top of the Seat on one of the larger elevator platforms, surrounded by guards, I scanned the sky overhead in nervous recognition. No wonder the demons of my city were worried. I counted at least three suns gone from the sky. Had they just been small, distant ones perhaps we could have kept things from the populace longer. But one of the major suns, tied to I didn't know which plane—that would be rectified as soon as possible—was so glaringly absent it was a wonder the crowd was as calm as they were.

There was a definite air of nervousness, but panic hadn't yet gripped the assembly. The fact they had come here on their own made me my own kind of nervous, but this had to be dealt with.

You can't tell them the truth, Ahbi sent. *They will stampede, Meira.*

Not all of it, I said as I mounted the top step and turned to face them. My power swelled around me and I grew in size, stretching upward into giant form until I towered over the parade. I felt Mabel's magic overhead and didn't need to glance up to know the shadow passing over was her drach form observing all from the sky.

"PEOPLE OF OSTROGOTHO," my voice carried, I'm sure, to the edge of the city so even those who weren't in attendance here would hear. "YOUR RULER SPEAKS."

They fell silent, the swaying crowd of hundreds of thousands of demons watching me with glowing eyes under the dwindling collection of suns. My heart pounded in my chest and I leaned heavily on Ahbi as I went on.

"DEMONICON IS UNDER ATTACK." I gestured, my power creating a three-dimensional hologram over the Parade, showing them the images of the Planeless gathering I snuck into in Bilhaeder, the face of Xeoniteridone. "The cult known as the Planeless seek to subjugate and control all demons." I pushed gently, at Ahbi's urging, against their hearts and minds, tapping into the power of Demonicon to reach them and felt them sway under my touch. Heady, this power I'd never used before.

I know, she sent. *Be careful.*

"There is a new nectar on the streets." I showed them Theridialis, the purple vial in his hand, as giant as I was though just a projection. "Resist it at all costs. Those who drink it leave themselves open to the influence of the Planeless."

The gathering swayed, their denial of such a thing so powerful I actually felt hope for the first time.

"You Ruler fights them with every ounce of magic," I said. "But you must also be vigilant and put an end to the spread of this nectar-borne disease."

You know, Ahbi sent, *maybe we should have done this ages ago.*

And Henemordonin would have had an aneurysm, I sent.

That would have been a pity. My grandmother chuckled evilly as I continued my speech.

"Trust in your Ruler and the Seat," I said, still leaning on the crowd. "Stand strong and accept no false offers of peace from false prophets."

"What of the suns?" The voice of protest was faint, and I was unable to pinpoint it. But somehow, it carried, sweeping past the gentle pressure of my coercion.

"TRUST." I hated to manipulate them, but I had no choice.

You don't, Ahbi sent. *Push harder, Meira. This has to end well.*

I tried. I really, really tried. But the moment I leaned in, felt them bend to my suggestion, the absolute worst happened.

The Node hiccupped. And the third largest sun above us flickered once and vanished.

No amount of coercing could do me a bit of good at that point. The gathered demons transformed from hopeful optimism to a frantic mob in the time it took for all of us to process the fact another sun was gone. The crowd cried out in a single voice of terror before surging forward toward the platform and the gathered court.

Toward me.

I started to shrink, desperate to orchestrate the escape of the court from the now panic-stricken demon horde, when the earth heaved beneath me. I thought at first it was me, that my anxious need to return to my normal size had unbalanced me. But the earthquake reached far beyond my own two feet, shaking the Parade and even the mountain itself. The crowd screamed, many demons falling under the pounding footsteps of the mob, weeping and wailing mixed with shouts and the crackling of magic as the gathering devolved into a blubbering mass of hysteria.

I spun to try to protect the others, only to find myself alone on the platform, the court long fled, my guards abandoning their posts in their own terror. Only then did I wish I hadn't insisted my friends remain above, feeling suddenly exposed and very afraid.

Ahbi's power crackled, forming a thick shield around us as the ground heaved again, tossing me to my knees. *Meira!* Her shout shook me out of my fear. *We have to get out of here!* I looked up and into the panic-stricken, furious faces of the wall of demons heading right for me. On instinct, I raised one hand, my power surging out to push them back, but it was too much. They were too much, their fear a wave of crushing force, beating me down into the still shaking ground, the platform stone cracking with a massive report under the stress of the earthquake and their terror.

They fell back as a shadow swooped low. Giant claws grasped me with delicate precision, caging me inside one huge talon before powerful wing strokes blasted the fearful demon crowd with wind. I gripped tightly Mabel's foot, staring down over the shrinking gathering as we gained altitude, unable to breathe as my chest heaved against my own panic.

Her magic cradled me as she transformed in mid-flight, depositing both of us in my quarters where I fell to my knees and sobbed.

Sassafras pounced on me, purring so loudly I knew he was as terrified as I was.

Demonicon was falling apart and I couldn't do a thing about it.

It wasn't often I could say Syd looked like crap. Usually, even when she was in the middle of taking apart the Universe with her bare hands, she radiated confidence and power, a firecracker of charisma my jealousy hated her for. But, when she arrived through the veil, Max beside her, only moments after my collapse, I looked up through my tears and saw, through her concern, just how tired and ragged she was.

And she made no attempt to hide her weakness from me, either, a fact that smoothed away the edges of envy and left me guilty—as usual—for feeling anything but love for my amazing sister.

Syd helped me to my feet while Max and Mabel conversed in their strangely layered and musical language. Her face might have been drawn with weariness, but her hands were as strong and steady as ever and I welcomed the touch of her skin on mine, even as I pushed myself to my feet, dashing the tears of fear and frustration from my cheeks.

She hugged me without a word, her arms tight, her body leaning into me as much as mine did to her. It felt good to support her even as she gave me respite from my worries, the world fading as our power connected at the most private level.

If this gets to be too much, Syd sent, *you tell me. I'll kill every single person who hurts you and then bring them back to life so you can kill them, too.*

I snorted a half-hysterical laugh in her ear. *Thanks*, I sent. *It's awesome having an all-powerful big sister. But you have your own problems. So if the Ruler of Demonicon can offer assistance at any point, you let me know.*

Family, Meems. Syd leaned back, still looking like she'd been dragged through a week with no sleep face-down in worry, but with a small smile on her full lips and a fresh sparkle in her deep blue eyes. *When it all comes down to the wire, the only thing that matters is the ones you love.*

I nodded, sniffling subtly, eyes burning with fresh tears that had nothing to do with the near-disaster outside the Seat. Her strong hands released me, but her power never did and I hugged her with my magic while Ahbi stayed quiet for once.

My sister shook herself, amusement gone, the narrow crease between her eyebrows forming, just like Mom's. For a moment, she looked like she was ready to keel over, give up and just toss her hands. But that instant passed and I knew, no matter what happened, Sydlynn Hayle would never quit.

Which meant, I wouldn't either.

"I was coming to fill you in on the veil crisis," Syd said, hands settling on her hips. "But I have a feeling your news is more urgent."

I let Syd feel the Node, the loss of the planes and told her of the gathering below. "There was nothing I could do," I said, voice cracking and warbling as my nerves returned. My nails bit into the palms of my hands, the pain bringing me back to focus. "I had control until the Node released another of the planes."

Which, Ahbi sent, a snap of power in her mental voice, *I'm certain was intentional.*

How can you know that, Grandmother? I eased up on my guilt and swallowed past the need to sob all over again.

Experience, she sent. *And the loss was just too much of a coincidence.*

Considering we all know there's no such thing, Syd's mental voice was dry and crisp, *I have to agree with Ahbi.*

"Which means," Sassafras said from his perch at my feet, "the Planeless are still in Ostrogotho and, if we carry this one step further, likely orchestrated this entire event for their own benefit."

It made sense, though my stomach churned from sickness at the thought. "We're losing, aren't we?" I hated to sound defeatist, but I could feel my world crumbling around me. And without a way to counter the cult, the loss of the planes, and the deterioration of the Node, I knew I was right.

Not even Syd was able to come up with a denial. "There has to be something we can do," she said, her frustration sparking in her eyes. She half-turned to Max who shook his head, diamond eyes dull. While he didn't appear tired like she did, there was a diminished feel to him I could only guess was the drach equivalent of weariness.

"I can pull none of my people from the repairs to the veil," he said, sorrow in his voice. "Even the loss of Mabel has had a detrimental effect. Though you, Sydlynn, have more than augmented our ability to heal the rifts between the Universes."

She shook her head, ponytail frizzy at the ends as static crackled across her shoulders. "We're just sticking our fingers in cracks," she said. "We need a plan to fix the veil completely."

Max sighed. "I fear, at this point, such a task may be beyond us."

They exchanged a long, silent look that had my worry meter rising by the second.

"Go," I said, pushing gently against her. "The veil is more important right now." How I wished things could be different! But Demonicon would survive, whether whole or in parts. If the veil between Universes fell... I had no idea the full implications. Syd talked of Creator's dark brother on the other side, how terrified she was of the thing Gabriel's gateway almost let through into our Universe. From the grim expression on Max's face, he completely understood what such a rift would mean and I didn't want to know what could make a drach afraid.

Syd groaned softly before throwing her hands in the air with a tsking sound. "I know," she said. "But." She crossed her arms over her chest, chewing at her bottom lip. "Meems, you have to take your power back from Henemordonin. There's no other way. You need to have the full support of Demonicon if you're going to have a hope in hell to fix this."

"She's Ruler," Sequoia said, voice soft and full of protectiveness for me while my mind sighed and wondered if our hope in hell was already long gone.

"But she's never really been Ruler, has she?" Syd's eyes narrowed. "I'm sorry, Meira. I know this isn't fair. But tell me, if you know—or if Ahbi does—how much your perceived weakness affects your control over the power of Demonicon."

Ahbi actually flinched inside me while I gaped at Syd with harsh denial in my heart.

A lot, Ahbi sent, shattering me completely. *It's part of the reason Henemordonin has managed to push her around. Meria's control of Demonicon's power is complete. But she can't access it fully until she is truly accepted by the court—by all of Demonicon—as Ruler.* My grandmother paused. *I'm sorry, child*, she sent at last.

So this is my fault? Rage roared to life inside me, battering against Ahbi, against Syd who held me with a sudden iron grip. I twisted in my sister's hold, fighting her maji power, so much stronger than mine. Sweat burst into life on my skin, the burning fury of my demon blood coursing through my veins. *DON'T YOU DARE BLAME ME FOR THIS, AHBI SANGHAMITRA.*

My grandmother retreated instead of fighting back. *It's my responsibility*, she whispered in my mind. *In trying to help you, in my selfishness, I hobbled your power and gave your grandfather the cracks he needed to destroy you. I see that, now.* I could feel her weeping, her tears washing away the burst of temper, sending my cracking rage into a hissing mist of regret and retraction. *Meira, I need to leave you before I make things worse.*

I felt her pull away, grasped for her on instinct and held her back. Maybe she was right and I should have let her go. But blaming her—or myself—for this mess was the wrong way to go. My temper cleared as quickly as it came when I met Syd's eyes.

"Only one person stands between us and success," I said. "Xeoniteridone has to die."

Sassafras snarled, but not in argument. "Cut off the snake's head," he said.

Syd nodded once. "You can handle that?"

I had to find him, first. But she didn't need to hear excuses from me. And I was done making them—and taking the blame. "I can."

My declaration—delivered in firm and determined voice—likely would have convinced her if the Node hadn't chosen that exact moment to wriggle, hiccup and sigh, releasing yet another sliver of Demonicon through its net of magic.

Syd flinched when it happened, eyes widening. Max's surprised grunt told me neither of them had really taken the problem as seriously as they should have.

"What," I said, unable to keep the sarcasm from my voice, "never felt a world fall apart before?"

Syd shook her head, cheeks paling, but I could tell from her dark expression, despite what she now knew, nothing had really changed.

"We'll have a look ourselves," she said, surprising me while Max nodded slowly. "If we turn up anything, I'll let you know."

"First priority is to stop the veil from imploding," Sassafras said. "Meira and Ahbi—and Mabel," the drach female nodded, "have already looked into the Node, Syd. And considering Abhi was once part of the network holding the demon planes together, I'm not sure what you'll be able to do."

Syd snarled silently before jabbing a finger at the

Persian. "Smartass cat," she said. "Fine." Her eyes lifted to mine. "Do whatever it takes, Meems," she said, backing up until she was side-by-side with Max. "But get that Node stabilized."

The veil tore behind them, the drach turning, his face elongating as he began his transformation. I watched them go, holding still and silent as my sister left, the gash sealing shut behind her while my heart pounded faster in my chest.

Ahbi, I sent. *Would you be able to do it? Stabilize the Node if you returned to it?* Why hadn't I thought of this before? It would be hard to let her go, but at least if she succeeded the Node would be safe.

She didn't comment for a long moment. *I don't know*, she whispered. *I don't think so, Meira. The Node itself is its own entity. I was already becoming part of it, rather than it becoming part of me, when I left it to join Ameline Benoit.* Her mind shuddered. *I was losing myself in the heart of Demonicon. And if I did become lost, I wouldn't be able to help you anymore.* I could feel how sad that made her, how afraid. *And when we tried to stop the exodus at the Node site, I felt it calling to me again, felt my will slipping away.* There were unshed tears in her voice, though her tone hardened and she fell still from her shivering. *What am I saying? I've grown weak, Meira, weak and fearful since I died.* Fire crackled between us. *Demonicon's safety—your safety—comes first. Take me to the Node and I'll do my damnedest.*

I hugged her fiercely, love for her surging inside me as I felt her travel through her terror at losing herself and back to the Ruler she had been, but better. *I won't send you to be sacrificed unless we know it will work.*

But it might work, she sent. *Let me go, Meira.*

Last resort, I sent. *There has to be another way.*

"Ruler," Sequoia's voice was so soft I almost didn't hear it over my racing pulse as I felt Ahbi acquiesce reluctantly. "What do you want us to do?"

The only thing I could do. "I need to take control of the court," I said, brusque though I felt quivery fear trying to rise. "Summon Rutorith at once."

chapter seventeen

The old soldier was my grandfather's creature, I knew that already. But with Henemordonin gone, maybe the demon would listen to me. I held myself still in the large chair I had Jabuticabron bring into my quarters, mimicking my grandfather's throne-like presence in his office, hoping to intimidate or, at least, influence Rutorith's opinion enough to take my armed forces back.

He entered reluctantly, flanked by several guards, while Sequoia glared and Jabut flexed his giant muscles in fury. But it was Mabel who faced Rutorith down most effectively, silent and staring from her diamond eyes, and I copied her demeanor.

He must believe you care not for his standing, Ahbi sent. *Who knows what your grandfather has told him to this point. Intimidation will not work with this demon. You must be firm and in command of yourself in order to impress him.*

I agreed with her assessment, though the fact I had to impress anyone actually pissed me off.

Good, Ahbi sent. *Use that. Do not, under any circumstances, let him push you around, or take no for an answer.*

Rather than challenge Rutorith about his little envoy, I settled myself into a false mask of stern leadership. "Assemble the troops," I said. "Ostrogotho will be placed under martial law until this crisis is ended."

"I don't take orders from you," he said in his gravel voice, not even using the honorific of my title. How far I'd fallen from my grandmother's day.

To hell with him, Ahbi snapped. *Kick his ass. Now.*

No, I sent, shoving aside my self-pity. *I'll handle this a different way.*

"You do," I said. "While Second Seat is your master, thanks to the laws he and his fake court have passed," I let that settle in a moment, though I knew it would have no effect, "when he is no longer available to command you, power reverts back to First Seat."

A hasty check on Sequoia's part told me that much, just in time, too.

Well played, Ahbi sent. *But I still say show him the might of Demonicon.*

He knows it already, I sent. *We both know he couldn't care less. I need to corner him and give him zero options.*

Rutorith frowned, his demons shifting behind him. "What have you done to Second Seat?"

Now that almost made me laugh. "If he hasn't fled the capital in fear like the coward he is," I snapped, "he's been taken captive by the Planeless." More shifting, and a whisper of fear this time. "You do know the guards you command are ineffective against the cult?" Rutorith stared at me, nostrils flaring. "In fact, there was an attempt at an attack on me last night in these very quarters." I showed him the images of the Planeless, letting him see for himself my cousin's face. That widened his eyes. "So, you tell me, captain," I sat back, steepling my hands before me, closing my eyes to disdainful slits, "where has Henemordonin gone?"

He didn't speak, jaw working.

It could be he really has no idea, Ahbi sent. *That Henemordonin duped him in some way. Lied about you to gain his trust. He's an old soldier, Meira. Rutorith thinks he's doing the right thing.*

An excellent observation, one I embraced as I stood and approached the new guard captain. "Rutorith," I said. "Our world is under attack and the demon you trusted to guide us through this crisis is gone without a trace." Well, maybe there was trace of him. I just hadn't looked hard enough. Maybe later. "Will you allow Demonicon to fall? Or will you, with your lifetime of service to the Seat and the demons of our world, keep me from doing everything I can to ensure the safety of our people?"

I had him. I could feel him cracking around the edges.

That bastard, Ahbi sent. *To twist the loyalties of an old soldier so badly he hates and mistrusts his own Ruler.*

One of his many crimes, I sent.

Rutorith seemed to make up his mind, eyes flaring with amber fire as he crashed one fist against his chest and bowed his head to me. "Ruler," he said in his unchanged gravel voice, "command me."

Battle won. Ahbi sighed in my head, satisfaction in her voice. *Well done, Meira.*

I gestured to Jabut who came forward immediately. "Coordinate with Rutorith," I said, even as the two demons glared at each other. "Pull Ostrogotho together before the whole city comes apart at the seams." It was hard not to turn my head, look out over the balcony, to the few plumes of black smoke rising from random sections of the city.

Jabut saluted, joined Rutorith as the old soldier left my quarters, face still troubled.

I turned from the closing door and faced my friends. "We need a way to counter the nectar." And to find Xeoniteridone. But I'd take this step first, and be grateful for it. "With Theridialis gone," I nodded sadly to Sequoia and Sassafras, "we need other options. Sequoia?"

She tilted her head before shaking it as she understood what I was asking. "I don't have my father's expertise," she said. "I'm sorry, Ruler."

"Any of the other scientists your father worked

with?" I was desperate, here.

Sequoia sighed, little hands wringing in front of her. "None of them have the skills Father does with nectar."

Zinnia, silent until this point, squinted at me as her long, thick lashes fluttered a little. "I may have a solution to the antidote problem," she said, sounding less than enthusiastic about her idea even as she went on, "but I can't promise you anything. My contact isn't exactly what you'd call reputable."

I had no idea what that meant, and I really didn't care. "We'll take what we can get," I said. "Set it up."

"I'd like to talk to Shenka," Sassafras said as Zinnia hurried from the room. "I'm wondering if she can get in touch with the Steam Union, see if they can shed any light on what's happening."

"Great idea." I reached for the veil and sadly watched as he slipped through. "Be back soon?"

"I'll be only a few minutes," he said. "Leave the door open." And he bounded through the opening, furry body dim in the low light of the basement in Wilding Springs on the other side. I watched him leap up the staircase before turning away.

"I must go." Mabel bowed her head to me. "When the Node discharged during your attempt to soothe the demons of Ostrogotho, I thought I sensed something. Perhaps I can uncover some truth if I examine it in flight again."

"Thank you," I said, genuine gratitude feeding my guilt. "You really should be with your people. I want you to know how much I appreciate your help."

Mabel smiled, white, even teeth sparkling in the light as she turned toward the balcony. "My place is here," she said, before morphing into her drach shape as she flung herself out the window. *With you.*

She had no idea how much better that made me feel.

"The Node monitors are no help," Pagomaris said as I turned back. At least she'd dropped her subservient act. I kind of liked her better this way, without the fake smile, though it still rankled she'd fooled me for so long.

Both of us, Ahbi growled.

"They aren't," I said. "How can you monitor something you don't understand the true structure of?"

"Because," Bakari said as he appeared from thin air, making me gasp in shock before aiming a kick at him for being such an ass, scaring me like that, "they, like most demons, have no access to their sorcery."

"Why then," I snapped at him, still furious for his lack of warning, "aren't your sect responsible for it?"

"Because it was never believed sorcery would rise again," he said. "Such power isn't required to maintain the Node now that it exists."

I waved him down, drawing a deep breath. "Secrets," I snapped. "Demonicon thrives on them. And will be destroyed by them, if this goes on much longer."

My door crashed open, the furious and power-charged form of my grandfather stormed through, his magic slamming into me before anyone could stop him.

"BY YOU!" He grasped onto my arm, jerking me toward the door as my magic rebelled, fighting him off. Trying to fight him off. Something had boosted Henemordonin's power, and, as he dragged me physically out into the hall, I realized with a burst of terror, he was stronger than me. I caught sight of Rutorith watching, though he frowned at my grandfather while I did my best to pull away. Had I gotten through to the new captain? It didn't matter, not when all the power of Demonicon wasn't enough to fight off Henemordonin. He had his own and, from the feel of him, the full support of the court. "And now, Senne Hathenemeira," my grandfather snarled in my face as he pushed me onto the elevator, "you will finally be held accountable for your failure."

Chapter Eighteen

The court had assembled and I could only assume my grandfather summoned them. Humiliation burned inside me as my grandfather dragged me down the center aisle between the staring gathering of family. Flashing red-tinted faces, glowing amber eyes, elaborate costumes and polished horns whipped past, blurring the features of those watching with almost identical judgment on their pinched demon faces. I stopped kicking and screaming, allowing Henemordonin to escort me for ego's sake, though he moved so fast I knew I had to look like an errant child being brought to task.

THE BASTARD! Ahbi writhed in fury, slamming against his power over and over again. *HE DARES!*

He did. And, by the time he pushed me with incredible violence to the ground at the foot of the throne dais, his power flattening me against the cold stone, I knew I was in serious trouble. And that he finally had me exactly where he wanted me.

I could feel the glee inside him despite his raging anger on the outside, refused to weep as his triumph added to the magic he used to control me, glittering amber eyes full of hate.

The court watched in silence, their judgment a weight I was used to bearing, though this time the pressure was so much I gasped for air. Henemordonin stood over me, one large index finger pointing at me as his outrage rippled outward over the family.

"This is the demon you have trusted to lead you," he boomed, voice carrying, fueled by more power. How was he stronger than me? Had I lost so much of Demonicon's support?

A better question, did I ever have my people's support? From the ease in which Henemordonin controlled me, the power of the planes unable to break me free, I had my answer. For the first time since Demonicon was formed, a Ruler was too weak to keep the First Seat. I feared the loss of some of the planes was to blame, but how did that explain his increased power? Surely the loss should mean he was weaker, too? Senseless, these thoughts as I whipped myself into focus.

It would have been easy to quit, to give up then and there and I was not ashamed to admit part of me wanted to. But I'd come too far, found my Hayle center again.

So, as my grandfather continued what I'm sure he thought was his epic speech, I stopped fighting and gathered my strength, searching for the means to escape him.

"Where did you go?" It was a meager challenge, my words, not backed by magic, but by doubt. If I could sow seeds of mistrust...

"I have been investigating this disaster," he roared at me, sweeping his arm over my head as he spun back to the court. "I left the Seat at great personal peril to do so."

EAT FIRE AND DIE. Ahbi was barely understandable. And I'm sure most of what she screamed in the back of my mind—as indecipherable as it was— was much harsher than that little snippet I managed to comprehend.

"You admit, now," I said, same calm tone—how did I manage it?—same bits of doubt, "our world is in danger?"

His control of me faltered, if only for the briefest of instants. And in that instant, I saw my true strength. He hadn't adjusted his strategy to adapt to the new me. Despite our last confrontation, Henemordonin didn't expect me to be rational. He wanted me to overreact, give him reason to take me down. But I wasn't playing his game anymore.

I'd thought him subtle, once, manipulative. But the pressure he applied to the gathered family as he refocused his attention on control showed me something changed in my grandfather as well. Something I could use against him? Instead of a carefully controlled lure, he beat the court with power, forcing them to listen and accept what he had to say. They shifted forward as one, leaning toward him, a sea of colorful attire and eager red faces, glowing amber eyes locked and glazed, down to the last and weakest of them.

"I do," he said. "I was wrong." There was zero remorse or apology in the magic crushing the doubt in the court. "I now know, from personal observation, conversions to the Planeless religion are happening in the open and in vast numbers, all over Demonicon." He spun back to me, outrage mixed with a new feeling. I took his hint of worry at my lack of overreaction as a success and pulled my power tighter to me as he tried to compress me into breathlessness. "And what are you doing about it, Ruler?" He brought all of the magic he had in his grasp to bear on me, on the court, more pressure than I'd ever felt before. It was amazing to me the hard shell I'd formed kept me safe from being turned to pulp and powdered bone. "Making speeches," his over-the-top arrogance sliced the family like a weapon. "Lying to the people while our very existence is threatened."

OH NO, HE DID NOT. Ahbi's frothing rage had finally distilled into icy fury, sharp and bitter.

"I seem to recall," I said, struggling to make my voice

sound casual and natural, as if I wasn't being slowly driven into the solid rock of the floor but, instead, safely on my throne three steps above me, "I attempted to warn you several times about the Planeless. Your investigation was unnecessary and has wasted precious time."

I hoped it was enough, but he was ready for me this time. Henemordonin's face twisted as he gestured above me, filling the air overhead between the floor and the warded ceiling above with a holographic projection. I knew the city, the ugly angles and dull buildings of Ilogabon. My stomach clenched at the sight of the Planeless in their dark robes, the giant crowds of worshiping demons falling to their knees before Xeoniteridone. The court swayed, their terror rising and, even before Henemordonin spoke more of his lies, whether I'd warned them or not, I knew my grandfather had won.

"Your order for the Planeless to disperse, for their gatherings to be declared illegal," he stressed the words with contempt, "has done nothing." Spittle flew from his lips as he turned back to me, towering over me. "You have failed us, Ruler," he snarled. "And because of you and your weakness, Demonicon faces the greatest threat to our survival since the Node was created."

I could have argued. Ahbi did, in my head, about how if Dad's damned stupid laws hadn't put me in this position, if Henemordonin had just stopped being a power hungry asshat for five minutes, we wouldn't be in this position. It wouldn't have mattered. I could see it in their faces, the gathered court. There was nothing I could do to convince them this wasn't my fault.

Nothing, except do something about it.

Grandmother, I snapped as Ahbi's temper fired again. *I need you.*

What? The whip-crack of her words cut me, but I welcomed the pain.

We have to get out of here, I sent. *Out from under his influence. I need every scrap of power you can give me.*

Ahbi grunted, boiling energy surging into me. *Take it*, she snarled. *And make him choke on it.*

I had one chance at this. The moment he knew I was going to fight back, Henemordonin would make sure I failed. But now I understood how the power worked, maybe I could leverage a little faith to get me out of this mess.

With tight focus, I pushed back. But not privately. Openly and in the full view of the court. That caught some attention, drew eyes, broke Henemordonin's hold enough his power diminished. Just a little, not enough, yet. But I had confidence now and pushed harder.

Slowly, ever so slowly, I forced him back. Silent, the battle, sparks falling into absolute quiet as the court watched, their support wavering back and forth, from him to me, until I was on my knees. And then, my feet, fingers brushing at the front of my skirt, as casually as possible, keeping my face steady and calm though my hands shook from tension.

I didn't say a word to him, or to the court. I didn't have to. The moment I was upright, their support shifted. Had I impressed them? Perhaps. But from the snarl on my grandfather's face, I hadn't won just yet.

I strode past him, ignoring him, even as he shouted after me.

"Where do you think you're going?"

"To Ilogabon," I tossed back over my shoulder, radiating confidence and strength, enough to sway the family members closest to me as I went by. "Where you should be." I spun just before the elevator. "May I ask," I said as my magic triggered the lift. "If the city was in danger, why the hell are you here?"

He stared at me in impotent rage, the court's support now back with me even as the elevator dropped out of sight.

chapter nineteen

I was already leaping into a transport when I released my hold on my power enough to raise the shielding. Enough for Sassafras to yell at me.

WHERE THE HELL ARE YOU GOING? I felt him coming for me, knew he had to be with Sequoia. His sister radiated horror at what just occurred and I couldn't bring myself to relive what happened all over again. Not to mention the fact I was so over people yelling at me all the time. I lifted off and pushed out of the bay as I felt Sass's magic enter.

I'll be right back, I sent. *I have to see for myself.* I cut him off before he could argue, and knew he was arguing, probably loudly and to anyone who would listen.

Ahbi had fallen silent when we entered the transport bay, her fury turned to a simmering pot of bitterness.

Grandmother, I sent as gently as I could as I threw us

toward Ilogabon, trying to ignore the signs of civil unrest in Ostrogotho, unable to deal with both issues at once as we soared over the churning city below. *We'll deal with him later. Right now, as you're fond of telling me, we have to focus.*

I'm well aware, she snapped. *Which is why he's still standing.*

We both knew it was a false threat. Abhi swore a few times in a mumbled snarl before releasing her anger and hugging me with a fierceness that sent the small hull beneath me to bobbing.

You, she sent. *You will be the finest Ruler Demonicon has ever seen.*

Tears tingled, my throat suddenly tight. *If I don't get us all killed first.*

I would have fallen long before now, she whispered to me. *The old ways of ruling no longer serve, Meira. You have my gratitude. And my apologies. And my sympathy, too, for what that's worth.*

I hugged her back. *I can't do this without you*, I sent. *Please, believe that.* Because I did, finally. I really needed her.

We'll see, she sent. *Now, what's the plan?*

Um. A small giggle of pure hysteria broke through. *Not a clue?*

Ahbi sighed. *You're such a Hayle*, she sent.

More giggles, totally inappropriate, but doing me a world of good as the tension from my ordeal finally broke.

Gently with yourself, Ahbi sent. *You've been through a great deal in the last little while.*

I can't afford to be weak, I answered. *Neither of us can.*

No, she sent. *But you've taught me there's nothing weak about compassion. That caring for others is more important than caring for power. Because only the ones you love matter in the end.*

Had I? I pondered that truth even as a vast mind touched mine, shadows falling over the transport when Mabel spoke.

I am here, she sent, distress in her mental voice. *Sassafras is very worried.*

I'm fine, I sent, the lie an easy one. *I'm going to Ilogabon.*

And I go with you. The drach settled in beside me, the sweep of her wings buffeting the small transport. *You should have summoned me*, she sent. Was Mabel actually showing more emotion? Or was I simply becoming accustomed to her stoic drachness?

We are capable of caring, she sent, softly chiding me.

I am so glad of that, I sent back, hugging her with my energy. She very gently, massive magic held in check, hugged me back. *And to have you here with me.*

The trip was a short one, forest and a low rise of mountains flying past below. As Mabel and I circled the city, it was clear Henemordonin hadn't made up the images he'd shared. The entire populace—or, it looked that way—stood in a mass outside the furthest building, circling a small podium in the middle with a sea of demon bodies. It was easy to spot Xeoniteridone on the stage, his whiteness bright and a clear target.

Shall I roast him? There was no humor in Mabel's voice.

Yes, I sent, surprised at my own fierceness. *But not here. Too much collateral damage.*

I can be specific, she sent. *But I see your point.* Xeoniteridone was surrounded by demons, suddenly, a flood of robed followers engulfing him.

The hard way, then. I opened up to the power of Demonicon and projected my face above the crowd.

"THIS IS AN ILLEGAL GATHERING," I said, my massive countenance echoing back toward me as the power of my voice rippled the robes of those below. "DISPERSE AT ONCE OR BE ARRESTED." How I hated it was an empty threat. I was alone—save for Mabel, of course—and I could see from careful examination a multitude of my guards were among the converts below.

What I wasn't expecting was Xeoniteridone's reaction to my orders. I assumed he would keep himself safe, protected in the surrounds of his followers. Instead, he detached from them, rising into the air, his white robe billowing around him as he grew in size, a soft, sad and benevolent smile on his face.

"You come with your creature of destruction," he said, voice low, but carrying easily, a powerful counter point to my demand. "You come to bully those who would live in peace and harmony." He turned his back on me, on Mabel, looking down on the worship of the gathered p-population of Ilogabon and gestured over them with the staff in his hand. "My children," he said, "do you accept such orders?"

"NO!" They spoke as one, a million demons screaming at the top of their lungs even as I reached for them, forgetting for a moment there was nothing to find. Just emptiness, powerlessness. And the devouring dark of sorcery, humming beneath everything.

Xeoniteridone turned to me, his caring smile full of sorrow. "You see," he said. "No matter what you do to us, we are free of the evil of power hunger, free of the need to harm our fellow demons. Free to be at one with each other and this plane."

What a load of... Ahbi spluttered. *Mabel, kill his ass.*

We can't. I felt my heart sinking as the crowd below cried out as one. Xeoniteridone's name. Over and over in a worshipful chant while he watched me.

Meira is correct, Mabel sent. *We have no idea what it will do the demons below. If he controls them and we kill him, we could harm them irreparably.*

And he did control them, through the charisma he radiated, so powerful it rivaled the magic of Demonicon.

Don't kid yourself, Ahbi whispered. *He's stronger than we are, Meira.*

"You can end this strife," Xeoniteridone said. "You can choose to join us, Ruler. To create a new, bright future for Demonicon and all demons." I had first felt the touch of his coercion back in Bilhaeder, when we originally met. But I'd somehow managed to break free and his power no longer affected me. That didn't stop him from trying again. But even as his magic slipped around me, a noose tightening, it slipped free and fell away while the monster inside me roared defiance.

Meira, Mabel sent even as I felt the darkness below begin to surge and grow, *we have to leave here, now.*

Leave? I'd never heard Ahbi so aghast. *We can't leave! We have to kill Xeoniteridone. This may be our only chance.*

The monster that was my demon blood felt the hunger of the sorcery coming toward us and reacted with a ravenous need of her own. The transport bucked as the power of Demonicon fought for control from the sudden seizure of magic, the monster within howling her fury at being shoved back. The dark of the sorcery below, triggered by Xeoniteridone, called to her, called to me and I felt the transport begin to fall even as the surge of black rose from the gathered demons to meet me.

Wind buffeted the transport, shaking me free momentarily from my monster's focus on the call of sorcery. Mabel's wings swept so close to my little ship, I rocked to the left, almost losing the shielding holding me in the air. I met her sparkling eye, felt her anger rise at last, the engulfing, world-shattering massiveness of it turning away from me and toward Xeoniteridone.

When Mabel roared, the entire gathering of demons fell silent, staring up at her. Her voice carried, shook the ground, made the very air vibrate to the point I struggled to stay aloft. But I was free, at least, from the sorcery calling to the monster within, and able to take control at last as the drach's furious protest finally died away.

They held still another heartbeat below, still staring, the silence deafening, almost painful to my ears. And then, in a surge triggered by mass hysteria, they turned as a single body and ran away. I watched the blossoming flower of fleeing demons expand outward, looking up, too late, to realize Xeoniteridone was long gone.

Meira. Mabel's magic buoyed me.

I'm all right, I sent. *Thank you.* My body shivered without my participation, a cold sweat breaking out over me. *If you hadn't been here…*

I was, she sent. *And I will be from now on. We must return to Ostrogotho.*

My power surged, the little transport joining her as she spun and headed back the way we came. And do what? How could I combat what I'd just witnessed?

Talk with Max and Sydlynn, Mabel sent, mental voice grim. *If we don't find a way to stop Xeoniteridone now, there will be no hope for Demonicon.*

And yes, I'd known we were in trouble. But hearing

her say it, the last of my hope died with the setting of the
remaining suns.

chapter twenty

My intention to storm in the court and my grandfather the moment I arrived back at the Seat was thwarted when I reached out to try to find Syd.

And encountered Zinnia instead.

Ruler, she sent, mental voice crisp against mine. *I must see you immediately.*

I really had to speak to Henemordonin, to diffuse the disaster he was creating around me. But her tone was so urgent I acquiesced.

Where? She showed me the stairway at the top of the mountain, the very one she'd led me down the night the Planeless tried to capture me. I saw her clearly, two figures in shadows behind her.

Your quarters, she sent. *In your closet.*

Such a rendezvous location should have made me laugh. But the deadly seriousness of her tone tied into what I'd just witnessed and the worry I lived with in an almost constant state these days held back any humor before it could emerge.

I'll be right there. I reached for Mabel, only to have her mind press softly on mine.

Forgive my eavesdropping, she sent. *We go.*

I actually didn't mind, to be honest.

Perhaps, the drach sent, *our arrival should be more private, though.* She tilted her huge head at me, diamond eye glittering in the glow of the rising moons. *Zinnia didn't seem to wish anyone to know she was there.*

Agreed, I sent. *Ideas?*

Of course. The huge drach headed for the ground and I followed her immediately. As my transport touched down, Mabel transformed into her human shape, coming to my side to help me out of the thin hull. "The veil," she said, her power tearing it open.

Why didn't I think of it?

"You have much more on your mind," Mabel said, gesturing at the gash, as though still in my thoughts. "And I am here to serve."

I shivered at the very idea one of the first race thought she served anyone.

Just take the help, Abhi sent. *Let's get this over with so we can go back to kicking your grandfather's ass over the edge of the mountain.*

I abandoned my transport, stepping into the veil,

Mabel at my side, her smooth, warm skin on mine as she took my hand. The trip was swift, the other side open and waiting already. I crossed into the dark quiet of my closet just as Zinnia appeared through the sliding panel in the back of the room, the same two shadowed figures behind her. I raised my hand in greeting while Mabel resealed the veil, the glow of the edges of the tear now gone and plunging the room into darkness.

My eyes adjusted as I tapped my power, the light from them casting amber as Zinnia bowed and approached.

"My Ruler," she said, voice low but clear. "I've brought the one I spoke to you about."

If only I could remember what she was—

She was bringing an answer to the nectar problem, Ahbi snapped. *Pay attention, Meira.*

She had no right to be short with me, but I forgave her. Partly because she was right.

Two hoods swept back, two faces revealed. I couldn't control the brief flinch of denial crossing my face at the sight of the small, ragged demon with one off-cast eye or the taller, if robust, older demon with the oily smile and two gold-capped fangs.

"Ruler," the second one boomed before Zinnia could glare and jab him in the ribs. He held up both hands, flashing with jewelry, his slicked black hair receding from a wrinkled brow though his eyes sparkled with good humor. "Forgive me," he said, the decibels dropping if not the charisma he poured into his words. "I am merely in awe at the honor of being in your presence."

I rolled my eyes and sighed at Zinnia. "What is this?"

She unclenched her teeth and shrugged elegantly, her robe twitching around her. "The best I could do," she said. Zinnia held out her hand to the skinny, misshapen form of the first demon, his thin hair waving around his protruding ears, horns shrunken and shriveled. When he smiled, his entire face was lopsided, but he bobbed a bow to me and, when he spoke, I found myself staring in shock.

"My Ruler," he said in a voice like velvet, reminding me of Sebastian DeWinter, the leader of the vampire clan back home. "I understand you're in need of a chemist."

"This is Portlish," Zinnia said.

The crooked demon tried a bow while the larger one, clearly in charge of the pair—or, at least, appearing to be—inserted himself between Portlish and me. "And I," he said with grandiose greasiness, "am Frestendel." He patted his paunch with one hand while the other lifted to slide over the slicked back patch of his hair, teeth flashing. "Portlish's... business associate."

Nectar dealer, Ahbi snorted. *And cook.*

I focused on Zinnia, stomach churning. "Have you lost your mind?"

She shrugged again, not smiling. "I told you there

might be an issue with this, Ruler."

Frestendel opened his big mouth to say something, only to have his cook slip forward and hold out one hand. I looked down at it, noting how well-manicured his black nails were, how soft his skin, how steady he seemed as he spoke again in his velvet voice.

"Zinnia has told me what you need," he said. "I can't promise you anything, but I can do my best. Making nectar is my livelihood, Ruler. And while I am no Lord Theridialis," I was impressed he knew of my friend, "I will do what I can to counter the poison."

"Poison?" I nodded to him to go on. "It's just a suppressant, isn't it?"

He dropped his hand, wandering eye rolling in its over-large socket. "I thought so at first," he said. "I, too, have been looking into this new nectar."

"On my orders," Frestendel said, pushing his stomach forward as if needing me to notice him.

"Correct," Portlish said. "You must understand, any new strains of nectar must be investigated."

"You create illegal versions for the use of the masses," I said. "Why do you care if someone else does the same?"

"Business, Ruler," Frestendel said. "And any nectar that suppresses the power of our customers…" He shuddered. "It's killing my bottom line."

At least they are honest, Ahbi sent.

I felt myself relaxing. "Tell me what you've discovered."

"The poison eats away at demon power," Portlish said. "Not just capping it, but feeding from it. The odd thing is, though," he scratched at one wiry eyebrow, the springy hairs jutting out in random directions, "the power isn't leaving them. It's going deeper."

Feeding their sorcery, Zinnia sent.

Which means Xeon's main goal isn't to suppress demon power, I sent, *but to waken their dark magic.*

She didn't comment. Nor did Ahbi or Mabel, both of whom I knew were listening.

"Can you counter it?" There had to be an antidote. I couldn't imagine Ram was trapped with the Planeless forever.

"I've been trying," Portlish said. "But my facilities are limited and I've had very little of the pure source to work with."

Frestendel again put himself between me and his cook, this time beaming a smile that had a definite edge to it. "We would be happy to help our illustrious Ruler," he said. "Demonicon's fate is in our hands." Arrogance oozed from him even as he tried for humble graciousness. "And we will do all we can to make sure the demons of our home are saved from this terrible drug." I heard Portlish sigh and resisted doing so myself.

"Thank you," I said.

His smile fell, sadness on his face, so false I almost laughed. "We have but one problem, my dear, dear Ruler," he said. "A matter of survival."

Zinnia's power snapped and Frestendel flinched, but he didn't move.

He has guts, Ahbi sent. *I'll give him that.*

No, I answered. *He has greed.* I could see it all over his face as he went on.

"Some small compensation," Frestendel said. "For the saviors of Demonicon."

I crossed my arms over my chest and leaned toward him. "Can you promise me you will solve the issue?"

"Of course." He beamed again while Portlish choked on a gasp. Frestendel glared at his cook a moment before returning his smiling attention to me. "We promise."

Brave of him, considering there was no way he could be sure his cook could come up with a solution. Time to show him what promising a Ruler would mean. I caught Portlish's eye and nodded. "If you find a viable antidote," I said, "you can ask me for anything you want."

"Anything?" Frestendel's eyes lit up and I could practically see him licking his chops in anticipation of his demands.

Like I cared. "Anything," I said. "But."

He froze, smile tight. "But?"

"If you fail." I let my arms drop, the power of Demonicon rising to swirl around me. The wind from its movement pushed the dealer back into Portlish. "Don't fail, Frestendel."

He swallowed hard, spluttering. "I assure you," he said, one hand gripping Portlish's arm, "we will not." He turned to his cook, shook him slightly. "Will we?"

CHAPTER TWENTY ONE

I left Portlish in Theridialis's lab with Mabel while Zinnia escorted the protesting Frestendel out of the Seat.

Watch him, I sent to the drach as the cook almost passed out from excitement.

Who will watch you if I do? Her diamond eyes flashed with power as I retreated.

I'll be fine, I sent. *I'm going to kick my grandfather's ass now.*

Best of luck, Mabel sent. *Let me know if he needs roasting.*

I did laugh then and hoped I wouldn't need her after all. *I'll send Sequoia down when I find her*, I sent. *Until then, make sure he doesn't steal anything and take off.*

I think this one is more honest than his counterpart, Mabel sent, mind still firm on mine as I stepped onto the elevator platform at the back of the room and took the short ride up to the throne room. *He will not give me trouble.*

The platform settled, the thrones just ahead from my

access from the back. I could see the court, the dais, but couldn't hear clearly what was being said and could only assume Henemordonin was droning on his usual garbage to the family. *Stay with me*, I sent to Mabel as I stepped around the side of the dais and looked up at the thrones.

And froze while the court stared at me in absolute silence. I barely noticed them. In fact, I forgot to breathe thanks to the sight before me.

My grandfather sat on my throne like he owned it.

Ahbi lost it, completely and utterly, while I did my very best not to shatter into a million furious Meira pieces.

"SHE RETURNS." Henemordonin jabbed one big finger at me. "The false Ruler has come back, in time to tell us why Ilogabon is no more!"

Meira! I caught Sassafras's connection, but barely, as though from a great distance. My eyes flickered over Henemordonin's lap to a side table next to him. A cage.

And the silver Persian inside.

"What have you done to stop the loss of our planes?" Henemordonin's heavy disapproval was fed by the same from the court. I caught my breath while my mind scanned the room for my friends. No Sequoia, no Jabut. Not a trace of Elph.

Where were they?

Meira, Mabel's voice cut through my shocked silence. *Do you need me?*

Her concern was enough to break me out of my stillness. *Maybe*, I sent, though I knew there would be nothing she could do to help me in this fight. *I'll keep you posted.*

I turned away from my grandfather, facing the court, stepping into the center aisle to address them directly, mind churning with what to say even as my grandmother's fit became harder and harder to ignore. I yelled at her once to get her attention, but she was nuclear and I knew there was nothing I could do about her.

"I've been to Ilogabon," I said, surprised how steady and calm my voice was while the court watched with gaping mouths and speculative whispers. "I've only now returned." I stood very still, head up but power contained, if only to keep Ahbi from blowing us both into bits in her rage. "I've confronted Xeoniteridone with the aid of the drach, Mabel." Let them remember I wasn't without support. "And I have felt the rise of sorcery in the demons who have converted to the Planeless cult. Sorcery they are using to destroy our world."

You're guessing, Mabel sent.

They don't know that, I sent. "If a way isn't found to stop Xeoniteridone, Demonicon will be no more in a very short time." I turned at looked up at my grandfather. "We must work together. This strife between Second Seat and Ruler has to end, or we will all end because of it."

I felt them sway toward me. Was it my calm again?

Maybe, maybe not. But from the look on Henemordonin's face, he felt it, too and there was no way he was letting me get away with it this time.

He's ready to act, Sassafras sent, just barely audible. *Meira, be careful!*

I hardly needed his warning.

"Tanasharia!" Henemordonin gestured. "Come forward, Lady, and tell us the truth of this matter."

My eyebrows flew to my hairline as my cousin stepped out from the gathered family. The last I'd seen of her, she tried to capture me, one of the Planeless, converted to the way of the cult. And now, here she stood in her court finery, a nasty smile on her face.

"If our Ruler wasn't so weak," she said, "this disaster would have been long averted. In fact, I am witness to her weakness." She pointed at me, spite in her every word. "Not only did she fail to take down the Planeless, she's been conspiring against her own Second Seat, our beloved Henemordonin, all this time." Beloved! Bile rose in the back of my throat. I wanted to slap her so badly I felt Ahbi's rage breaking through and had to rein myself in.

Tanasharia gestured with one hand, showing a holographic scene I knew all too well. Only this time, it wasn't my quarters and she wasn't one of the Planeless. Instead, the dark-robed cult members encircled Henemordonin's bed and swooped down on him. "She works with the cult itself," Tanasharia's voice rose to an accusing shriek. I watched in growing frustration as her little show climaxed into Henemordonin bursting from his bed, a heroic figure who scattered the attackers with ease. I knew then it was a fabrication.No demon could stand against the sorcery of the Planeless, even as the last image flashed—showing me

standing in the corner of his bedroom, scowling, cloak just showing the outline of my face before the hologram died.

All kinds of arguments rose in my mind, battled to be spoken first. That Henemordonin could never have stood against the sorcerers, how it would be foolish of me—so foolish—to be in the room myself if I really ordered the attack. That if I wanted Henemordonin dead, I could simply have him killed.

I felt myself losing control of my mind, while Ahbi's rage grew and grew. I opened my mouth to speak and felt her flow outward, my sight suddenly tinted amber as my grandmother fought for control. She lashed at Henemordonin in pure hate, using my power, the power of Demonicon and her own to slash at him. He must have been prepared, because the blow bounced from his shields and ricocheted back, rocking me on my heels.

GRANDMOTHER! I screamed at her in my head, fighting for control. *STOP! YOU'RE MAKING THINGS WORSE!*

I WILL KILL HIM! She slammed herself against me, only the surge of drach power from Mabel's interference stopping my grandmother from striking at Henemordonin again. *HE WILL DIE IN FLAME AND AGONY.*

Ahbi Sanghamitra. Mabel's deep voice carried so much power I staggered, knees jerking under me, my grandmother's wavering form appearing outside of me a moment before snapping back into place. *You must stop.*

She sobbed as she beat against the drach. *Let me go,* she screeched. *Let me go!*

We held her together, crushing her down as she fought until she could fight no more. When she was done, she gave in, turning her back on me, spinning what was left of her will into a ball and cutting herself off so completely it was as if she'd never been with me at all.

I gasped for air and looked up, sweat trickling down my face, into Henemordonin's triumphant eyes.

"You see," he said, voice tragic, magic rippling with regret. "You see for yourselves the mistake we've made, that one so young, so conflicted, could ever take the First Seat." How dared he use such a tone with me? Chiding me as though I were a child.

Steady, Mabel sent.

I pointed at Tanasharia. "She lies," I said, though my words emerged as a whisper of denial. "She is one of the Planeless." I reached for her with my power, to prove it to them, that she was no longer in possession of her demon magic.

And felt the familiar tingle of fire as her power surged against me.

I could only gape at her, then, as Tanasharia pushed back, unable to resist in my utter shock.

"You are the one who lies," Henemordonin said. "You are the deceiver. And I can only hope we have discovered your deceptions in time."

I have to do something, I sent to Mabel, my desperation clawing at me like a wild animal.

You can do nothing now, she sent, sounding far less upset and much more curious than I expected. Oddly, her attitude calmed me more than I ever thought possible. *We must regroup and consider.*

I can't just walk away from this, I sent, even as my grandfather stood and pointed at me.

"Senne Hathenemeira," he said. "I challenge you for First Seat."

We knew this was coming, Mabel sent even as Sassafras broke through.

Fight him, my demon cat sent. *But be careful.*

I braced myself, was about to accept—and gladly, in all honesty—when Tanasharia spoke again.

"By law," she said, grinning openly at me now, "a full consensus on removal and replacement of Ruler requires no challenge." She turned to curtsy at Henemordonin.

201

"Isn't that correct?"

The bastard. He'd set all of this up, and more. I watched hopelessly as he nodded with false thoughtfulness.

"You are right, Lady," he said before raising his gaze to the court. "A vote, open and clear, so there can be no dissention later the choice was manipulated in any way." He was such a liar. I could feel him leaning on them even now. "All those in favor of retaining Senne as Ruler, state your intention."

If Demonicon had crickets, they would have been singing in the silence. My heart and soul shriveled while no one—not a single demon—would meet my gaze.

You expected otherwise? Sassafras sighed in my head. *I'm sorry, Meira.*

"Your silence is telling," Henemordonin said. "And now, all those in favor of ascending me, your Second Seat, to the Rulership of Demonicon, make your intention known."

Their decision was hardly a shocker, though I did note about a third of the gathered court didn't vote at all. Still, the remainder showed enough enthusiasm for the regime change to send my last hope plummeting to my feet.

Hardly Ruler four years and now, in the time of Demonicon's greatest need? Nice going, Meira.

"So let it be," Henemordonin said. His power reached

for me as focus shifted toward me. "Relinquish the magic of Demonicon and step down."

"We do agree," Zinnia said. Where had she come from? My head spun around as I heard her voice, as did the rest of the court. She gestured at Henemordonin with indifference. "But with concessions."

I think that surprised him and, as my father's ex-fiancé looked around herself, I saw the curiosity in the others.

"Senne Hathenemeira might not suit Ruler's seat," she said, "but she is powerful, more powerful than any of us." Murmurs of assent. What was she up to? "And, by Demoniconian law—unless I've missed a shift in that ruling, too—demands the most powerful sit on the thrones of our world."

Second Seat, she whispered in my head. *He was able to control you from there because of his new laws. Maybe you can do the same and turn the tables on him.*

I could have hugged her right then and there.

But Henemordonin must have seen exactly where this was going. "Accepted," he said, the court nodding in agreement with him like the damned puppets they were. "But, with a final concession, my family." They returned their attention to him and away from Zinnia. "Due to the absolute disaster we face, I would ask all new laws be reverted, and that we return to the original laws of our world until this crisis has been averted."

So mercurial their support, and so easy the collapse of demonocracy. Their nods of approval, bobbing horns and headdresses, proved to me once and for all the ruling class of demons on Demonicon deserved what they got.

I'm sorry, Zinnia sent. *I tried.*

No, I sent, mind churning as Henemordonin focused on me. *You've given me more than I expected from this. We'll figure it out.*

My grandfather's power latched onto me. "Now," he said. "Release the magic of Demonicon and bow to your new Ruler."

I let it go, though not without deep and aching sadness. It didn't want to leave me. The power fought my release, struggling against my grandfather, its disgust at the feeling of him. But I gently detached it from me, like letting go of a crying child, and sagged just a little as it rose from me and assimilated into Henemordonin's magic.

It was so hard to watch the power go, spitting and hissing at my grandfather, though I knew its initial rejection of him wasn't lost on the court. Their discomfort was nothing compared to mine, though, and for the first time, I truly understood how Ahbi felt.

All will be well, Mabel sent as the magic left me, her power buoying me up. *Your people are obviously unwilling to remove you completely until Henemordonin proves he can save them. And when he cannot, it is likely they will turn to you, again, for help.*

I couldn't even bring myself to hope she was right. Instead, I pointed at the cage next to Henemordonin. "Release my friend," I said, struggling a little to care past the empty feeling inside at the loss of the magic of Demonicon.

"He is a known accomplice of yours," the new Ruler said, settling into his throne once again. "A conspirator in the downfall of Demonicon,"

"He is mine," I said, quiet, but finally showing my anger past the gaping hole. My anger at last, not Ahbi's. "And I am your Second Seat." How it choked me to say those words. "If you don't trust me or those I care about, replace me now."

He didn't have the courage. At least, I could hope not. But even my arrogant grandfather must have known his perch on First Seat was perilous, because he finally gestured and nodded with benevolence I knew he didn't feel.

"Very well," he said. Sassafras snarled at him and hopped down, sashaying his way toward me as though nothing had happened. I bent and lifted him into my arms while my grandfather spoke. "As a show of good faith."

"You know nothing of good faith," I snarled. "And you've made this mess. So have fun cleaning it up." I spun and left, knew everyone stared and didn't care.

Find Sequoia and Jabut, I sent to Mabel. *Zinnia, my quarters.*

chapter twenty two

Elph waited for me at my door, his anxious face brightening as he saw me stomping my way toward him. I felt a surge of relief at the sight of him, partly because I worried about his safety and partly because it made me hope my other friends were fine, too.

I set Sassafras on the floor, the Persian's tail beating against the cold stone and was startled when Elph wrapped his arms around me and hugged me tight.

"I'm glad you're safe," I said. "Where are the others? Were they captured?" I could only think of Sassafras in his cage and shivered at the thought of my friends being held captive.

"I'm fine," he said. "I hid from the guards when they came to take me prisoner." His lips brushed my cheek and I sank into him. "I was more concerned for you," he whispered in my ear. "Are you all right?"

I leaned away, nodding, the battle for control almost lost as tears welled in my eyes. Now the massive momentum of horribleness was over, I felt myself threatening to come apart at the edges. Instead, I pushed him back and jerked my door open, barging into my own suite as though an enemy stood on the other side.

Empty, even of Pagomaris, my life constant. Surely she was fine? A member of the Daeva, she could have easily escaped. Still, mental images of my friends all hurt or even dead—despite knowing it was melodramatic and unlikely, even for Henemordonin—I couldn't help the despair building a crescendo around me. A thin wail escaped before I could stop it, weariness falling on my shoulders. I found a seat and sank into it, hands on my face, as though that physical act could hold back the floodwaters of despair I fell into.

Hands touched my shoulder, my knee, Elph's gentle magic supporting me. "It's going to be all right," he said. "You're still Second Seat."

"You were there." My words mumbled out from under my hands.

"I was," he said, voice full of sorrow. "They'd stopped looking for me by then and I was able to sneak in and watch. I'm sorry I couldn't do anything to stop it."

"No one could." Sassafras's tone was far different, a crackling mass of fury. "Henemordonin saw to that."

I let my hands drop, exhaling all the air from my

lungs. My eyes caught the angry cat's, and I found it very hard to care he sizzled with magic, his tail beating against my leg, his ears flat back. In fact, it was hard to care about anything except my failure.

"He won," I said.

"He did," Sassafras said. "This round."

I sat back slowly, body aching with the need to quit. "Sass," I said, slowly as the truth sank in, "I don't think you understand. He not only has the power of Demonicon," I shuddered, feeling the ache soul-deep, "and the First Seat," the image of him sitting on my throne made me want to throw up, "he got the court to agree to repeal the new laws. No more demonocracy. He's a dictator and can do as he pleases."

"All true," Sassafras said, practically spitting each word out of his cat mouth. "So what are you going to do about it?"

I shook my head, body sinking further into the chair as reality finally settled on me in absolute understanding. "Nothing," I whispered.

Sass didn't say anything as Elph held my hand, thumb stroking the skin in slow circles.

Screw them all. Why should I stay here and fight for any of them when they abandoned me like this? My effort to raise my anger failed. I shrugged and spoke aloud what I was thinking. "I'm going home." That was that. I was actually quitting. And I couldn't muster a scrap of regret to combat the choice.

"For the best," Sassafras said, voice suddenly reasonable. "I agree completely."

I met his eyes again, sadness burning my throat. "I know Syd will let me rejoin the coven," I whispered around the tightness. Wanting him to argue with me while he shrugged his cat body back at me.

"If that's what you want to do," he said, "I think it's a great idea."

It hurt so much to hear him say that, almost more than losing to my grandfather.

"It's fine," Sass went on, turning his back on me. "It's too hard, I get it. You were never trained to lead, not really." What did he say? Air gasped into my lungs. "You were always subordinate. I suppose it's too much to ask now for you to stand up when you were never taught to do so." How could he say these things to me? Elph hissed at him while a tear escaped, a traitor drop of hurt and loss, to trickle down my cheek.

"Do not speak to her that way," he said. "She's doing her best."

Sassafras spit, growling deep in his chest. "No," he snarled. "She's not. She's never given her best, ever. And that's a character flaw I didn't foresee." He stood and faced me again, eyes narrow slits of fury. "But that's all right," he said, voice settling once more. "I know the perfect person to take care of this mess. Your sister will clean the floor with Henemordonin and find the right demon to sit on the First Seat. Since you aren't that demon."

My shriveled heart burst wide, flooding me with a rage so powerful I was on my feet and howling before I could stop myself. Sassafras didn't retreat, staring up at me with those same lidded eyes, tail twitching as I slammed into him with power.

"SYD SYD SYD!" The carpet under his furred paws smoked as my magic crashed into his shields, absorbed into the plush covering in massive sparks. "I'M SICK OF HEARING ABOUT SYD!"

"Then step the hell up," Sassafras said, cold and sharp. "Or go home."

The fury washed out of me as fast as it rose, leaving me gasping and near sobs. "You goaded me on purpose." I was such a fool, of course he had. I wasn't seeing anything clearly right now.

Sass's paw touched the toe of my boot, his ears twitching as he relaxed his furious stance. "Meira," he said. "You know none of what I said was true. You'd be long gone if it were."

I choked on a sob. Was he right? Knowing Syd was out there, better than me… but no. He pushed me and I let him.

"You are the one we need," Sass said, tone finally gentle as he opened his power to me and let me feel his heart. "What do you think will happen if you leave? To Demonicon?" He wanted me to care, that much was clear, but how could I bring myself to muster any kind of desire when it was obvious those who controlled our world didn't want me?

"None of this is Meira's fault," Elph said, still sounding offended. I realized then he continued to hold my hand and squeezed back even as I rejected his attempt to protect me.

"It is," Sass said. "She was Ruler. This happened on her watch. And now, if she walks away, there's no one left to fix it. You think Henemordonin can?" He snorted, paw dropping to the floor. "We're doomed, Meira. Unless you can find a way to stop Xeoniteridone. And we both know it."

I didn't respond. There was nothing I could do. Henemordonin had won, beaten me and no matter how much I wanted things to be different, this was the reality of my life, now.

"I won't leave," I said. "I'll do my duty. But I have no idea how to stop him."

"If you're ready to stop pouting," Sassafras said, "and take some action, for the sake of the elements, instead of reacting to Henemordonin and Xeoniteridone, maybe we can finally make some headway."

"I thought I was," I said, sinking into my chair again. Hope was long gone. Sassafras could talk all he wanted, but without a light at the end of the tunnel…

"Your biggest problem," Sass said, "is being confident and just acting."

"Like Syd is confident." My foot itched suddenly to kick him.

But Sassafras's laugh disarmed me. "No, silly," he said. "I wouldn't go that far."

A tiny chuckle of my own escaped, though I didn't know where it came from. I certainly didn't feel like laughing.

"Your strength has always been thinking things through," Sass said, leaping up into my lap at last, his tail wrapping around him in a furry circle. "You lost that when you became Ruler. And your lack of ability to trust your instincts and your logic has led us here."

He was right about that much. My first impulse upon becoming Ruler had been to replace Henemordonin. But I'd allowed him to remain, and that mistake cost me now.

"I don't want you to stop thinking," Sassafras said. "Your sister's lack of foresight and thought of consequences isn't the only way to solve problems. One Syd is enough, thank you—use your brain." A white paw pressed to my hand. "But when your plan is complete, act without hesitation." Sass sighed and shook his head. "I know you feel like you're stuck in a corner with nowhere to turn. But Meira, if you're right about Xeoniteridone and the fact he's using the sorcery of his converts to take the planes apart, we have to deal with it. The more demons he recruits and controls, the faster things will deteriorate."

I hugged him on impulse, releasing Elph's hand so I could embrace the demon cat fully. My nose tickled, his fur hot under my skin. "I can't do this alone."

"You won't have to," he said. "And that, my dear Meems, is your final strength. You are a team player and always have been, unlike your sister. So assemble your team and don't see using them as a weakness. Because it's not."

I released Sass who remained where he was, looking up at me with perked ears and quivering whiskers.

"Thanks," I said, my heart beginning to heal even as a seed of an idea grew inside me. "Xeon is using sorcery," I said. "And all demons have access."

Sass nodded while Elph took my hand again. I smiled at him, a tiny smile, but with returning confidence.

"What do you have in mind?" His amber gaze held steady on mine.

A frown pulled at my brows. "I don't know for sure," I said. "But I do know if I'm going to find a way to fight Xeoniteridone and his horde, I need to access my own sorcery."

Sassafras gasped and then head-butted me. "And that," he said, "is the first really awesome idea you've had in ages."

chapter twenty three

I paced my quarters, impatient now to act as I waited for Zinnia to arrive. My attempts to reach Syd—even with Mabel's help—failed miserably, though I didn't want my sister's help this time. I just wanted to keep her posted. This job, finding a way to fix things, was mine and mine alone.

But, no. Not alone. I clenched my hands into fists at my side as I paced, thinking of Sequoia and Jabut, my faithful Pagomaris. Where were they? I'd been unable to reach them and realized Henemordonin must have captured and imprisoned them much as he'd done with Sassafras.

Worry for them had me in a frantic state by the time the door opened and Zinnia entered. All of my concern collapsed around me as I looked up and saw she wasn't alone.

Sequoia hugged me with a soft cry. She was slightly rumpled, but didn't appear all the worse for wear. Jabut was another story, split lip and cracked horn telling me he'd put up a mighty battle. Pagomaris hugged me, too, though she seemed the least rumpled of the three.

"What happened?" I met gaze after gaze in a circle, focusing on my aide as she began to speak.

"They came for us the moment you left for Ilogabon," she said, her subservience still missing. "I tried to convince Jabut not to fight," her wry grin had nothing of humor in it, "but I might as well have asked a *pterys* not to stampede." The odd, five footed elephant creatures popped into my head and I nodded. Jabut looked contrite, at least. "I'd already broken us out and was on the way into the city with these two," she gestured at the brother and sister pair, "when you returned." Her face fell, elaborate hair dipping as she bowed her head to me. "I'm sorry, Meira."

"Don't be," I said, pushing down my own returning sorrow. "I'm just glad you are all right." I turned to Sequoia who hugged Sassafras to her. "I need your help upstairs in the lab," I said. "But we're going to have to shield what we're doing from Henemordonin." As long as he didn't know already Portlish was hard at work in the private lab under the throne room. "Mabel is guarding the cook Zinnia recruited to work on the nectar, but I need someone to watch him so I can free up Mabel." No way I

216

was admitting I wanted the drach with me at all times.

Sequoia bobbed a curtsy. "On my way," she said, already turning to go. I let her leave, Jabut escorting her, and focused on the two assassins. "Where's Bakari?"

"Here," he said, emerging from thin air, as usual. I didn't jump this time. I wondered if I would ever be capable of surprise again after the week I'd had. Bakari's face was lined with weariness and a good measure of anger. "You let him take First Seat."

My fist impacted Bakari's chest before he finished speaking. "So did you and your order," I snarled. "Now shut up and focus."

"He must be eliminated," Elph said, outrage ringing in his voice. "Can your order kill him?"

"We can," Bakari said.

"You can't," I snarled between clenched teeth. "Who do you think he'll blame if you fail?" No fear, not this time. Just practicality and frustration. "And if you succeed, do you think the court will ever trust me?"

"Do you care?" Bakari's bluntness was beginning to grate on me.

"If I'm going to save them from destruction," I said, "I'm going to need them to believe in me again. And murdering Henemordonin blatantly will ruin any chance of that." I shook my head. "I want him humiliated, broken, shown as the liar and manipulator he is. I want him to crawl on his hands and knees at my feet and beg me not to kill him while the entire court demands his death." My mouth filled with saliva as my monster woke, her hunger gnawing at my insides.

They all stared at me as though I'd grown a second head, but I couldn't care less.

"Now," I hit Bakari again, more gently this time, "tell me you've done your damned job and found Xeoniteridone. Him, we kill without remorse or hesitation."

Bakari's jaw jumped. "I'm afraid," he said, "we have as yet to locate him. Or he would be dead already." So much bravado after so much failure. I didn't bother mentioning Mabel and I had been unable to kill Xeoniteridone and, considering their past crash and burn, the Deava probably wouldn't be able to either.

I turned away from him and to Zinnia. "Go with Bakari," I said. "Find Xeoniteridone if you can and keep an eye on him if you do." I had no idea what we'd do then. Maybe call Syd, if I could reach her? Surely she could take him down, even if the rest of us failed. Or the combined might of Mabel and Max? There had to be a way to take the sorcerer demon out. I refused to believe he was untouchable.

I looked down at Sassafras. "Go help your sister in the lab." He nodded and trotted off, casting a look at me over his shoulder. Zinnia followed Bakari as the two faded into thin air. That left Elph and Pagomaris, watching me.

"Elph," I said, "I need your help, too."

"Anything," he said.

"I need you to follow Tanasharia." She was a tool of the Planeless, this I knew for certain. But, was she deceiving my grandfather? Or was he part of the conspiracy? I had to know. "If she's still working for Henemordonin, I need to find out if he knows more about the Planeless than is healthy for us."

Elph hesitated, glanced at Pagomaris. "I won't leave you alone," he said.

I gently kissed his cheek, stroked it with my fingertips. "Please," I whispered over his mouth as he sank into me. "I need someone I can trust."

He nodded once, swallowing hard before lowering his lips over mine. The kiss was soft, without power behind it, but it still made my heart quiver and my skin heat. I stepped back from him as he bowed to me and spun, striding for the door without a backward look.

When it closed behind him, I squared my shoulders and faced off with my aide. "That leaves us," I said. "Up for some digging into Demoncionian law?"

She came to my side, frowning a little. "You have an idea."

"I do," I said. "Henemordonin asked the laws be reversed to the original ones set for Demonicon. I'm going to take him literally." I hooked arms with

Pagomaris and headed for the door. "Hopefully there's something in the distant past that we can use to our advantage."

She grinned at me, amber eyes sparkling. "Clever," she said.

About time.

chapter twenty four

I suppose I should have expected my grandfather to be waiting for me in my office. But when I saw Rutorith standing outside the open doors, the sight of Henemordonin waiting within, I actually quailed. It was an old reaction, one I couldn't afford to take hold inside me. Desperate times pushed me to stride past Rutorith without a glance and down the three steps into the large space.

"You have your own office," I said, keeping my tone light as I brushed past my grandfather. "But if you want this one, I'm happy to have my things moved out by morning."

"Keep it," he said. "I could care less where you perch, Second Seat. That's not why I'm here."

"I really don't care what you want," I said, turning to face him with my back to my desk. Pagomaris hovered

221

near the cavernous fireplace, her subservient act back, if only for his benefit. My peripheral vision caught the influx of guards as Rutorith and some of his fellows joined my grandfather.

Now what?

"Your little display of anger in the throne room reminded me how much risk you place us in," Henemordonin said. I could be surprised, it seemed, and appalled. How could he manage to fake such concern when I knew it wasn't true? "Your grandmother's spirit controls you when you need to be in charge. It's clear now her influence is detrimental to the safety of Demonicon."

I felt Ahbi stir at last, though she didn't unfold and return to me. I let her hide, knowing it was best if I handled this without her volcanic temper getting in the way.

"Your opinion," I said. "But I think you forget, Ahbi Sanghamitra was the finest Ruler Demonicon has ever seen." Present company completely included.

"Was," Henemordonin said. I could feel the power of Demonicon in him, but it was dull and sad. I wished I could simply wrestle it from him and destroy him. "The operative word, Meira."

I shrugged. "So?"

He held out a sheet of parchment, the words glittering with magic. "I plan to petition the court to have her spirit removed from you," he said. "It's an old law, but one I'm within my rights as Ruler to enact."

Ahbi rolled over, misery radiating from her. She'd given up on me as much as I'd given up on myself. But I didn't have time to comfort her as a thread of panic rose.

"And do what with her?" I refused the piece of parchment, ignored it as he dropped it and it floated to the floor.

"Allow her to pass on, of course," he said, as though benevolence was natural to him. "To let her spirit finally rest."

To strip you of her power, Pagomaris whispered in my mind.

And her help, I sent.

I couldn't help the disdain in my voice, on my face, as I scowled at him. "The planes are literally falling apart around us," I said, "and you're being a petty, controlling idiot."

Henemordonin's brows pulled together. "Whose fault is it Demonicon is facing this crisis?"

"The court isn't here to be impressed by you now, Grandfather," I said. "You don't have to try to twist the truth. We both know it's yours." I tossed my hands in the air. "If you'd just pulled your power-hungry head out of your ass long enough to see I was trying to save our people, and backed me up even a little, there's no way Xeoniteridone would have been able to do what he's done." I was pushing the truth, but he'd backed me into a corner and I was tired of his crap. "And we both know it."

I have no idea if my grandfather would have finally admitted he was at fault. He never had the chance to comment either way. The moment I finished speaking, I felt something impact me from behind, shoving me forward and onto my knees.

One look up told me what was happening through a wash of robes as the room flooded with Planeless converts. I caught sight of Tanasharia's grinning face while Henemordonin spun and ran, Pagomaris fighting to reach me.

My cousin lunged for me, blackness enveloping me as her demon magic retreated and her sorcery, the emptiness of it eating me alive, crushed me into unconsciousness. But not before I heard her parting whisper.

"Should have just stayed home, Hayle," she said.

And darkness.

Black sighed around me as I opened my eyes. My mouth tasted thick, mind warping as I reached for consciousness. Where...? My fingers weren't working properly, my arms and legs not answering my commands. The world shifted sideways, then back, my stomach heaving against the movement while the dark continued to dominate my vision.

Someone sighed and muttered and I reached for her automatically. But I couldn't find her—who was it? I knew it was a she—only a deep pit I seemed to fall down and down and down—

My body heaved, rolling sideways, vomit spewing from my mouth, burning my throat, the taste of bile harsh on my tongue. I coughed, my chest tight and painful as I tried to pull myself together. What happened…?

Snippets of memory, of Tanasharia and Henemordonin, Pagomaris calling my name in desperation, the touch of a vast and worried mind… Mabel. Where was Mabel?

Where was I?

Throwing up helped to clear my head a little, the bitter aftertaste almost familiar past the reek of vomit. Chocolate?

Another sigh, a snore. Not in the room. In my head. In my…

Ahbi.

My power swirled in me, looking for her, making me sick all over again. But I refused to stop looking until I found her. Found her. Yes, there, still curled into her ball of rejection, but now asleep. And no matter how I prodded her, my insides warbling and protesting, she remained unconscious.

I pushed against her even as my power retreated from

me, the fire element burning to a cinder, hissing into an ember, dying in a puff of smoke. Panic grasped my chest in a vice, squeezing me as I fought for the magic I'd spent my life with, all of my witch power dissipating like dust in a breeze, gone from me.

All of it gone from me.

Powerless, I gulped air in the dark, hands clawing at my face, desperate need digging deep inside me.

And finding the monster within.

I embraced her where always she'd terrified me, if only for access to magic, any kind of power, anything at all. And fell into a giant, empty pit of blackness so engulfing I screamed into the dark.

And came back the rest of the way to clarity, even as my veins began to burn, the familiar feeling I fought for years, the hunger, not for power, but for nectar, surging to life again as I finally understood why I tasted chocolate.

Nectar raced through my system, killing off my hope, my ability to fight. I writhed where I lay, body aching with the need for more even as I wept and screamed into the darkness where my monster lived.

Despair like I'd never felt in my life shattered my spirit into dust and left me there to die—

She bends over me, her amber eyes on fire with excitement, the nectar poised over my lips while I weep and beg her for more. The deliciousness of it as it passes over my tongue while my soul cries out in hurt so deep I know I will never survive its pain. Hours and days and minutes of agony, bliss, agony, bliss as she feeds me nectar, flavors like chocolate and cinnamon and spicy fire burning the lining of my mouth but I don't care, will never care for anything ever again except Sekaniphestat and nectar and the call of my addiction—

My eyes snap open, my hunger encompassing. I must feed immediately.

There is light, a face hovering over mine. I know her. Tanasharia. She doesn't have what I must find. Fearless, ravenous, I try to sit up, but I'm bound by something, held in place. Distantly I'm aware of my body, of pain, though it's so far away I barely feel it as I fight for freedom.

Her face retreats, replaced by another. I know him, too, his white hair falling over one shoulder as he looks at me. Tanasharia is beside him, worry in her eyes. I care less for her fear, focus on him.

Maybe Xconiteridone can give me what I need?

Their lips move and they speak to each other, their words sounding underwater, far away, undecipherable while the monster in me snuffles around for escape. I've fallen still, there is no use in harming myself if they are going to give me more nectar. I wait, impatience growing, flickers of another face superimposed over Tanasharia's. And older, beautiful face, one I flinch from, associating her with pain and need. But seeing Sekaniphestat's countenance reminds me again of the burning in my veins and a moan of desire escapes me.

My eyes roam the room, settle on a handsome demon on my right, just behind Xeoniteridone. The name *Ram* rises to my lips, parched and cracking. My tongue rasps over the damaged skin, loud in my ears. He watches me with empty eyes while my heart whispers to me of love and other things that don't matter anymore.

"Please," I whisper, a shout in my head. "Please."

Xeoniteridone's smile makes my stomach quiver in hope and despair and disgust. I can't hear him yet, not clearly, but the shape his mouth makes looks like, "Soon."

No, not soon. Now. NOW.

Tanasharia retreats again, replaced by a hated face. I claw at him immediately, sharp pain bursting in my wrist as I damage myself. My grandfather pulls back in horror, but I can't break free to kill him, to grasp his neck in my fingers and squeeze out his life.

"Traitor," I hiss at him. "I'll kill you."

Fear crosses his face, much as it did Tanasharia's. I laugh, the sound harsh in my head, my body bucking under the restraints. My hand comes free, flopping on my stomach. I've hurt it too much to make it function normally, but I don't care. I'm free and I will kill him and drink his blood, surely as sweet as any nectar.

The monster howls her need, lifting me from the platform where I lay, the strap across my chest groaning against my ribcage.

When I land hard again, panting, my gaze finds one final face, but this time it stops me cold. Elph's sweetness and intense caring is gone, replaced by repugnance. He despises me, it's clear in that moment, crystal shattered into a million fragments of pain lashing me, cursing me, taunting me I'd been such a fool to trust him.

And now, my need to kill shifts from the traitor Henemordonin to Elph, even as my ears finally unstopper and the brilliant clarity of the sounds in the room hits me like a blow.

"—do with her now?" Henemordonin is talking, a sharp edge to his voice, almost whining. "Kill her?"

"Don't be a fool," Xeoniteridone says. There is no hesitation in him, not even a little, his control as deep as the blackness of his sorcery. My monster strains to feed from him as he holds her off with ease. "We should have done this all along." He finally frowns, aimed at Elph. "Maybe if you'd done your job, this wouldn't have been necessary."

"I tried." More whining, but Elph's is younger, full of bitterness. "You both acted too soon before I could convince her to trust me. Don't blame your mess on me. I was doing my part."

"Decades of work wasted." Henemordonin turns

away, hands in fists.

Decades. "Traitor," I whisper again, unable to stop myself.

Xeoniteridone bends over me, smiling. "Oh, my dear," he says. "You have no idea how long I've worked to attain my goal, how I fought to cast off the controls of those who created me in order to fulfill my destiny. But none of that matters now." He sits on the platform, his face over mine, body blocking most of my view. I now know it's not nectar I crave as much as the power he has to offer as his charismatic magic flows over me, into me, pulling at the monster inside me. She lunges for him only to have him block her from feeding on him. "Now you will be one of us, won't you, lovely Meira? And with your help, we will be able to fully establish the church and complete the fracturing of the planes ahead of schedule."

I stare up into his pale eyes, not caring my world is at risk, only wanting. Needing.

"Please," I whisper one last time.

Xeoniteridone strokes my cheek with one finger, his love engulfing me. "Of course, my dear," he says, other hand lifting a glass bottle full to the brim with deep purple liquid. "Is this what you wanted?"

My lips part as he pours it into my mouth and I fall—

Mother's milk, sweetness and light spiraling into darkness and need—

Monster roars. The air bursts with fire. Blackness eats

me, flashes of vision like slides from an old projector penetrating the massive power of the dark.

Flash.

Terror on Xeoniteridone's face, pulling away, frozen in the moment.

Flash.

They are screaming, falling back from me, I'm above them somehow, shadow falling across them in a blackout shaped like a nightmare creature.

Flash.

Slick, hot blood on my fingers, delicious on my tongue as I lick them clean.

Flash.

Fresh air, the sky above, brilliant moons and stars.

Flash.

The monster.

Meira.

Meira no longer.

Need roars into the night sky and shambles into the dark.

Chapter Twenty Five

Monster starves, scuttling from a dark corner toward the scent of chocolate. She must feed. Two demons huddle in an alleyway, a bottle between them. They scatter, screaming in fear as Monster leaps on them, letting them go.

She doesn't want to hurt them. They are irrelevant. The bottle of nectar is almost empty, but there is enough—just enough—to send thrills of fire through her veins. The darkness swallows it, demands more, more, always more.

She goes in search of a larger source. Stomps through an underground nectar den, ripping apart furniture, sending demons scattering, tossed, broken dolls of flesh and bone while she crouches behind the counter of the run-down bar and opens the tap to the barrel of nectar, swallowing as much as she can as it coats her in the thick fluid.

More.

Monster stumbles into the street, hurt turning her with a roar toward a group of demons attacking her with magic. She leaps on them, the blackness unsatisfied by the nectar pulling power from them. This is what she really wants, what she must have. They go down beneath her, three giant guards, unconscious, drained to the quick.

More.

Always more.

She runs from the others, too many, though they are unable to harm her now. The dark is vast and devouring, though it knows even Monster can't take on dozens at a time. She dodges into the night, escaping to the edge of the city and out into the plain beyond.

A smaller grouping of buildings calls her, a town outside of the towering spires behind her. She prowls, still starving, knowing she will never fill the gaping blackness but unable to stop herself.

A small demon child emerges before her, screams and runs from her at the sight and, for a moment, Monster almost pulls her back. To take her power and devour it. But the sight of the terrified child snaps inside her, driving her to the darkness between buildings where she sobs into her hands, choking on tears.

The need snaps her out of it like the crack of a whip. Monster's head comes up, the taste of power—a great deal of power, so delicious—close and coming closer. She leaps onto a rooftop, sniffing the air for the scent of so much magic, trying to find the source.

A shadow passes over head, blotting out two of the moons and making her suddenly afraid.

Meira.

The voice, the name, stirs something inside Monster. Something she never wishes to uncover. She embraces the darkness and throws it at the shadow over head before leaping into the alley again and running.

She should stay and eat, refresh herself with the massive power behind her. But her instincts tell her to run and she runs.

A small, silver creature appears before her, hissing, spitting, amber sparks flying from shaggy fur.

Meira!

No, she must escape, she can't stop. The blackness shoves him aside as she dodges past him and toward the openness of the plane beyond the town. She will find other places to feed.

A giant blocks her way, diamond eyes sparkling like stars. He is massive and Monster grows to meet his size, roaring at him, cornered despite her fear. His magic is delicious, she feels the taste of him already but when she tries to feed from him, she meets a rainbow wall she cannot penetrate.

"Meira," he says in a deep voice that fills her with

terror.

Monster spins to run from him.

Finds herself face-to-face with a human woman.

"Meira," Syd says.

And the world shatters.

I opened my eyes, just like that, the sight of my canopy overhead making me frown. In bed? What was I doing in bed? I had something to do.

Didn't I?

Syd leaned over me, the heavy, silver body next to my face, on my pillow, rumbling with a purr so loud I could barely hear my sister as she spoke.

"Meems," she said, tears sparkling in her eyes. "Welcome back."

And then.

Everything.

Crashing on me, over me, through me and I sobbed a giant cry.

"Syd!" I clung to her, shaking, body aching, my left wrist on fire with pain. My memories returned in waves of guilt and regret, self-hate and loathing until I didn't think I'd ever draw another breath.

But I did, if only to sob again.

Meira. Ahbi's voice whispered to me. *My dear, you're safe, now.*

AHBI. I hugged her, or tried to. Only then did I

understand.

"My magic." I pushed Syd back, more grief taking hold of me, crushing me until I wished I would just die. Just die already.

Syd's fingers brushed my forehead, Sassafras's purr rising in volume. I felt his magic, and the stirring of the monster all over again, but when she tried to feed from the cat, from my sister, Syd's magic blocked it.

"It's suppressed," she said. "But your sorcery is wide awake."

"The monster," I whispered, choked around tears. "That's what the monster is." So I'd had my sorcery all along.

"I believe so," Syd said, sitting back. "Weird, right?"

I stared at her in hurt shock. "Weird? Is that all you can say?" I died inside over and over at each memory, of what I'd become before she rescued me. Of what I could be again, so easily…

No, Ahbi sent. *Never again, Meira. You control it. Not the other way around.*

"I can't do this!" The wail cut me to the bone, the truth more painful than anything. "I want to die, Syd. Please, let me die."

My sister nodded slowly, her face sheathed in tears as she quietly wept, both hands clinging to my unharmed one. "I know how you feel, Meems," she whispered. "I really, really do. Of anyone, I understand."

She did, of course she did. Hadn't we fought to keep her with us when we thought Gabriel had died? "How did you bear it?" I didn't want to and this was different. Had to be different. Because if I let go, I proved to myself I was weaker than her.

Syd's fingers tightened. "You and Mom," she said. "Max and Sass. Gram. Shenka." She swiped at her cheek with one shoulder, the t-shirt material already dark with moisture so these weren't the first tears she'd shed. "I would never have survived without you holding onto me. Never." Syd released a shaky sigh. "I'm the last one who will blame you if you want to go home, Meems." My sister leaned forward and kissed my forehead. "We'll take care of you, the coven. Heal your heart, your soul, if we can. And I'll keep you safe, I promise."

One last sob ripped me in half before I fell back on my pillow and let my tears flow while Ahbi's power hugged me. It took a great effort to keep my sorcery—the monster—from feeding on my grandmother, enough effort I was able to pull myself together, at least enough to think.

"How long?" I looked down at my wrist, twisted it and winced at the pain, though it wasn't so bad, not like I remembered.

"Almost six days," Syd said. I gaped at her, let my hand fall to the covers.

"Demonicon." I gasped the word, realizing then there

would be no retreat for me. As kind as her offer was, as much as I wished I could be that girl who hid and let others protect her, heal her, I wasn't. I was a Hayle witch. And, damn it, I was the true Ruler of Demonicon.

Bravo, little heart, Ahbi whispered.

"The degradation slowed," Syd said, one hand pressed to my shoulder to hold me down as I tried to rise. "We're not sure why."

Maybe I knew. "Xeoniteridone was there," I said, voice cracking. "I may have hurt him when I freaked out." The flashing images of my snap-shot memory showed him falling back from me. Had I killed him? I could only hope, though that hope was slim. "Enough to slow him down, maybe."

"Meems," Syd said. "What happened?"

I told her what I knew, which wasn't much, though more and more came back to me as I spoke in warbling whispers. "This reaction was way stronger than the old one," I said. "Whatever the new nectar did to me, it wasn't what they were expecting."

"Perhaps Sekaniphestat's formula triggered something in you that reacted against their nectar," Sass said.

"No," Syd shook her head. "I have a feeling it was something completely different. Meems, you and I—and Dad—are the only demons I know who've stripped another and woken the monster."

Sass cleared his throat. "You're forgetting someone."

She stroked his fur. "Right, sorry. You too, Sass."

"What does that have to do with anything?" My brain still felt muddy, the hunger of my sorcery a gnawing, constant distraction. Now that I'd chosen to stop focusing on my grief, the monster stirred and demanded to be fed.

"What if the real reason you reacted the way you did was because your sorcery was already awake?" She shifted her position, fingers tapping on her jeans as she mused. "They weren't expecting such a strong reaction, I'm sure of it. Maybe they have a more controlled way of waking the blossom, instead of feeding something already open and hungry."

It made sense to me, even as the monster snarled. "Which meant they couldn't control me. They fed her and gave her what she needed to grow."

"Exactly." Syd snapped her fingers, nodding.

"I can't access my demon power." I winced as the monster struggled.

I can use mine, Ahbi sent, even as her power formed a shield around the gaping sorcery. It took a bit of a struggle, while Syd watched with narrowed eyes but didn't interfere. I wrestled my sorcery down, trial and error pushing against Ahbi until the monster finally sighed in frustration and retreated.

If we work together, Ahbi sent, sounding winded despite the fact she had no lungs, *not only do we have access to demon power, but sorcery as well.*

"If," I said. "What if I can't control it?"

Syd shook her head, patting my hand. "You have Mabel," she said. "And me. And you're stronger than you think you are." Syd's smile was hard, fed with anger, though not at me. "Look at what you survived, Meems. More than survived." She grinned, showing teeth. "They'd better look the hell out."

ChapTER TWENTY SIX

They greeted me with hugs, kindness, softness I really didn't deserve. Jabuticabron looked so hurt and lost I finally hugged him back. Sequoia wept as she kissed my cheek, even Zinnia's pain clear on her face. The only one who didn't show worry was Bakari, but I didn't expect it from him.

Mabel's embrace swallowed me, the heat of her and the surge of her magic making me feel safe enough to cling to her like a child. When she released me, a single sparkling tear tracked from her diamond eyes.

"Forgive me," she said. "I have failed you, Meira."

"You have not," I said, turning to face them all, still at her side. Max stood behind Syd, Pagomaris hugging herself next to Sequoia who cradled Sassafras in her arms. "No one was at fault. Except." I shuddered, teeth clenched against my need to run. "Xeoniteridone.

241

Tanasharia." They all nodded. "Elphremantic." A few gasps, though Jabut looked grim enough I knew the false suitor's days were numbered while I suddenly wanted to go scrub my lips with a caustic cleaner. I'd let him kiss me, fool me into thinking he cared, and consider him over Rameranselot. He'd die for that. "And Henemordonin."

"First Seat was involved?" Sequoia's eyes flared with amber fire.

"He was," I said. "He is working with—or for, for all I know—Xeoniteridone and the Planeless. Decades, he said." I ended with a whisper. "I'm a fool."

They tried to protest, but I shut them up with a slash of one hand.

"I have work to do," I said, retreating into duty while Syd nodded once. "Pagomaris, I know it's no longer your job. But I need to look like Ruler when I face the court."

"No," Syd said, stepping forward. "Let them see you now, as you are." I looked down at myself, how my hands shook, the thin fabric of my robe. "Let them see you are stronger than they ever thought possible."

They followed me, my friends, my sister, the drach, as I left my quarters for the elevator. Jabuticabron rushed on ahead, his sister with him while Sassafras settled in Syd's arms, to summon the court. They were already assembled, though it was late at night, looking haggard and lost, whispering as I appeared and walked without my usual false confidence down the center aisle.

I stopped at the bottom of the dais, turning to face the gathered family while my friends hung back and watched, waited for me to do what I had to do. Suddenly, faced with the fear of my court, I didn't care what happened to them, what they thought of me, even if they agreed.

With slow deliberation, I turned and ascended the steps, sinking at last into First Seat. And not one of the gathered demons said a word to stop me.

"The one you would allow to be Ruler," I said, "has betrayed you all." I showed them—or, Ahbi did—using a hologram of my own, letting them see what I saw, hear what I heard. As the memory replayed, my grandfather's face and words echoing through the throne room, the court broke into wailing cries of fear. Even more so when I let the scene go on, forced them to live what I lived as my sorcery reached out without my bidding and shoved it in their faces. "Tell me, where is Henemordonin? Where has he been the last six days? Why has he, after all his conniving and posturing, left you, abandoned you?" My voice remained level, heartless, empty of emotion, as empty as I felt as I sneered at the waving feather headdresses and fake black armor, the polished silver spikes and elaborate hairstyles. Wastrels, pitiful and pathetic. It was so easy to allow disdain to rise and feed from their insignificant need to be noticed. "You care nothing for Demonicon," I said. "You care only for your petty power struggles and your needs of the moment. I'm so sick of you all, you're fortunate I returned."

They flinched from me to a demon, falling to their knees before the dais, some sobbing, others clawing at the stone floor as though trying to escape. But there was no escape for me, so there would be none for them.

I finally relented when the memories ran out, pulling my power back while Ahbi fell quiet. Weariness of spirit held me still, slumped in my throne, staring with contempt over the demons who had put me in this position surely as much as Henemordonin and Xeoniteridone. I listened with growing disgust to their weeping, hated them so powerfully it was tempting to allow my sorcery to strip each and every one of them to nothing.

Only the steady, watchful gaze of my sister held me back. That, and the Hayle witch in me, her compassion almost burned up. I tasted chocolate in the back of my throat and hissed in fury.

"This," I snarled, "is your fault."

They looked up at me, a mass of terror.

"Our world is dying," I said, "because of you."

More wailing, begging for forgiveness I would never give.

"I should leave and let you burn," I said. "Let Demonicon fall because you," I sat forward, jabbing a finger at them, "trusted him," I pointed up at the hovering image of my grandfather, still held in place by my sorcery, "over me."

More begging. Let them. Just let them.

Meira. Ahbi's voice was gentleness over steel. *What do you want to do?*

I don't know, I sent.

Neither do I. She sighed, not a trace of anger in her. *After all I gave them, this is what we've become. Maybe it's time Demonicon died.*

Maybe. I met Syd's eyes, her steady, confident presence.

And made my choice.

"I may not possess the power of Demonicon any longer," I said. "But I won't let you stop me." I stood from my throne. "I will save this world, with or without you. But I swear to you," I walked down the stairs, releasing my sorcery , "if any of you stands in my way again," the flinched back from the black power flowing out of me, "I will devour you whole."

They bowed as a group, their platitudes of undying loyalty lost on me. I passed them, passed Syd and Mabel and my friends, heading for the elevator.

Meems, Syd sent. *I'm sorry. Hell of a way to grow up.*

Trial by fire, I sent to her as I kept moving out of sheer will. *Welcome to the club.*

I made it to the elevator, starting the way down as

Ahbi's magic controlled the platform with Syd and the others beside me. A tingle next to me was all the warning I needed as Bakari materialized from the air even as I turned to face him. His surprise equaled my satisfaction.

"Sorcery," I said. "You'll have to teach me the trick, now."

He bowed his head to me while Syd scowled at him. "My pleasure," he said. "But it will have to wait." The tension in his shoulders told me there was far more at stake here than one-upping him at last. "There is something you must see."

I allowed him to take control of the elevator, easing Ahbi from her iron grip on the platform with a touch of sorcery. It was going to take some getting used to, but we were already working together far more smoothly than we ever had, so I felt hope return where once only ashes lived.

I held my questions as we fell to the base of the Seat, led from the platform and to the next elevator as Bakari strode off as though knowing I would follow. Syd bit her lower lip but kept her silence, too, and I was grateful she managed to do so despite her usual caustic nature.

When the platform finally settled far below the mountain, discharging us into a dark tunnel lined with cell doors, I shivered and finally spoke.

"Where are we going?" Syd looked equally as queasy as I followed Bakari down to the end of the hall, remembering then she'd spent some time in a cell like these.

"Here." Bakari came to a halt, the sound of scuffling behind the door, grunting and moaning pulling my brows together. What had he trapped in there, some kind of animal? Bakari paused, a brief, hurt look passing over his face before he gestured, opening the door.

I stepped past him, Ahbi ready with power as was I, but neither of us found it necessary. A dark figure strained against bonds both magical and physical, head down, hunched and broken-looking in the dim light.

"What is this?" I turned to Bakari, saw his jaw jump as Zinnia gasped over my shoulder. She rushed past me, into the cell, to crouch next to the demon who threw himself against his bonds.

It wasn't until she reached out to touch him he lifted his head, amber eyes empty of recognition but face as dear to me as any I understood at last.

"Ram," I whispered. All the anger I felt toward him for lying to me, all the pain and heartache over his betrayal fled at the sight of him as my love and fear flooded to the surface. I almost rushed toward him, only holding back when he moaned like an animal and bared his teeth at me. Ram strained against the shackles, his wrists bleeding as the heavy metal cut into his flesh. I flinched in sympathy, my own experience fresh enough I could imagine what he lived through and helping me remember to breathe past my need to hold him close and never let him go.

"They woke his sorcery," I said, hating the dull sound of my own voice, the hopelessness in it. I cleared my throat and tried again. "Hooked him on nectar." Now my words sounded detached, almost clinical, while my heart screamed in agony for him. Not a big improvement, but at least I wasn't about to burst into uncontrollable sobs.

"Indeed," Bakari said, just as distant. "We were able to capture him after you went missing. He was one of the Planeless we could only guess were searching for you. He's been incarcerated here ever since."

Six days. "No sign of him coming out of it?" Six. Days.

"None," Bakari said. "We've tried feeding him nectar, regular nectar, to no avail. His sorcery is starving and, though we've fed him some power to keep him alive, I fear he will not survive much longer if we can't find a way to counteract his addiction."

I reached for him with my darkness and made connections I hadn't before. "It's not the sorcery holding him in thrall. It's the new nectar. He needs it."

"He does," Bakari said. "If it weren't for his addiction, he would be like you." His eyes settled on me, a look of speculation on his face. And was that hope for his son? "If we can find out how you managed it, perhaps we can save Rameranselot."

"My sorcery was already awake," I said. "But Ram's was, too, if he's one of you."

Bakari nodded.

"Then maybe it was one of Sekaniphestat's nectars that gave me the edge." I turned to Sequoia. "Tell Portlish. Dig up all of your mother's old formulas. The answer might be there."

She nodded, spun and left, Jabut guarding her even as I turned back and did my best not to go to Ram. For, I knew if I did, I would break again and I couldn't afford to do that.

"We need more answers," I said, a snarl on my lips. "This is too slow. I take it the cook hasn't come up with an antidote?"

Bakari didn't answer, which was answer enough.

"Xeoniteridone and his people are nowhere," Bakari said.

That was impossible. They had to be—

I gasped the same time Syd did, both of us turning to each other.

"They aren't here," I said.

"So they have to be there," she finished.

"Where?" Bakari finally showed temper, snapping at us.

"On the other planes," I said. "Stupid."

"Not stupid," Syd smacked my arm. "Busy."

She grinned and I answered her grin, unable to stop

myself.

"Sorcerers are able to travel the veil," I said. "We haven't been able to find Xeoniteridone because he leaves Demonicon and hides elsewhere."

Bakari snarled. "How then do we find them?"

Syd held out one hand to him, guiding him aside, winking at me. "Allow me to fill you in," she said.

I let her go, head down with the assassin who listened intently, and turned back to watch Ram continue to fight. My sorcery touched him and I felt him grasp onto me with desperation. I simply couldn't stand to see him this way any longer and, with empathy returning where I was sure it was dead, I gently knocked him out.

Zinnia eased her nephew's unconscious form onto the platform bed and met my eyes with hers brimming tears. "We have to save him," she said.

I approached, sank down next to the demon I was sure I'd marry someday if I could convince him to love me. He looked about as horrible as I felt, cheeks hollow from starvation, skin pale, eyes sunken. He continued to writhe even in unconsciousness, his need flowing over me still.

A disturbance at the doorway turned me to face Portlish as he slipped inside with a bottle of nectar in his hands. I flinched back from him, only to realize the scent of berries and cream did nothing to me.

Nothing. Where once a craving so powerful I could

barely stand it lived, now there was emptiness as vast as the sorcery I controlled. Knowing my addiction was gone brought tears to my eyes and I couldn't react for a long time, even when Portlish bent and pried Ram's lips open, trickling the concoction into his mouth.

Ram bucked beneath me, eyes snapping open as he screamed, the nectar dribbling out and over his cheeks. I held him down with sorcery, glaring at the cook who observed with tilted head and a slow, bobbing nod as though Ram were some experiment and not a living demon.

"What did you do?" It took more to put the damaged Ram back to sleep, a harder push I feared would hurt him. Portlish looked up, as if only noticing me for the first time, beaming a sudden smile.

"I think I know how it was made, now," he said, voice full of joy.

Meira. Only Ahbi's voice crackling in my head kept me from grasping the crooked little demon in one hand and squashing him like a bug. *We need him.*

Are you sure? I released my anger in a slow exhale, though it emerged in my voice as I spoke. "Maybe you misunderstood," I snarled, one hand on Ram's chest to keep the connection and force him under further. "I want an antidote, you idiot. Not more nectar."

Portlish's expression immediately altered as he bobbed his head to me. "Ruler," he whispered. "In order to counter the effects, I must first understand how it was made." He slipped a thin vial from within his clothing, the fiery red liquid throwing off glowing sparks of light from its interior. "I believe this is, if not perfect, as close as I have come."

I reined in my anger and sat back. "I'm sorry," I said. "I didn't…" My free hand slipped over my face as my weariness returned. "It's been a long week."

"I understand completely," the cook said. "I need to test my latest attempt."

Horror gripped me. "You've been…" I glanced at Ram, his hanging head as the sorcery of his aunt held him still. "You tested on him?"

"We had to," Portlish said. "There is no one else." At least he didn't seem happy about it.

I held out my hand on impulse, heart aching for Ram. "Then test it on me."

The reaction to my offer was immediate. Half a dozen voices, both in my head and out loud, shouted, "No!"

"Meems." Syd pushed her way to me past Mabel and Max while Sass jumped up on Ram's pillow. "Absolutely not. We just got you back."

"I need my power," I said, still holding my hand out. "If I'm going to beat Xeoniteridone I need access to everything I can get my hands on." I shrugged. "My nectar addiction is gone. I just need to cut the control of the stuff they gave me."

Syd shook her head, scowling. "Forget it," she said. And pointed at Ram. "Give it to him."

Bakari knelt beside me while I frowned up at my sister. "I won't let you test it on him," I said.

"We've been testing on him for almost a week," Portlish said, voice very soft.

"Please, Ruler," Bakari said, finally showing his fear to me while Zinnia wept softly beside him. "If it can save Ram..." He pulled himself physically together. "You can't be risked. And we need the information Rameranselot has in his mind."

The iron grip of Mabel's power settled around me. "It is the only way," she said.

It wasn't. And I was tired of not being the one taking action. But they were right and I had other things I had to do. If the antidote did incapacitate me, there was no saying what I'd do or how I'd react. And the thought of waking the monster again...

"Fine." I stood, shoved my way to the door, refusing to watch. "Just give it to him, then."

I only wished giving the command didn't make me feel like I'd sentenced the demon I loved to a fate worse than death.

chapter twenty seven

A massive shift in the Node almost knocked me to my knees, pushing me forward into the wall across the hall. Strong hands grasped for me, pulled me upright and I turned to find Mabel standing next to me. The vibrations in the ground didn't stop for a long moment while I felt—this time really felt—the Node shed one of the planes.

The veil tore beside her and I followed the drach through the gash before anyone could stop us. I felt Syd reach for me with her own sorcery, but the cut snapped closed behind her while Mabel shifted into full drach form, tossing me onto her back.

We emerged through a gaping hole into tearing air, the buffeting wind of the separation hitting Mabel hard and driving us toward the ground. I trusted her to recover, focusing on the city below as Bilhaeder began to shimmer and fade.

The air beside me tore and Syd and Max emerged. *We will focus on the Planeless masses*, Max sent in his massive mental voice. *You save the plane from Xeoniteridone.*

My sorcery stretched outward in response, touching the tearing edges. I felt where Xeoniteridone had begun the separation, seeing the thin line of black growing into a bubble trying to surround and segregate Bilhaeder's plane. Mabel roared as I threw my power against the pulsing sorcery and siphoned off the magic feeding it.

My own grew with a howl of pleasure, the separation halting and beginning to fail as the monster inside me drew on the power giving the thin sorcery the energy it needed to grow and expand. I felt Xeoniteridone then, his rage coming through the magic he focused on the tear and grasped his mind in mine.

I'd never felt so strong, not even when I had all the magic of Demonicon at my disposal. It shocked me enough I didn't kill him, at least, not yet, instead tearing open the way between us so I could see him in my mind's eye.

He was below me, somewhere in the city. A simple tug and he would be here with me—

He pulled free, and, in doing so, had to commit his power to fighting me. Last time I'd tried shielding the Node with demon magic, to no affect. Even Mabel's drach power had failed. This time, I had sorcery, the very power my enemy used to destroy the link between planes. I felt where his attention held the siphoning draw on the bubble of power between Bilhaeder and what remained of Demonicon and, instead of drawing from it, fed it in counter to his pull.

Xeoniteridone howled in fury, his magic countered in balance. I could see the warbling connection solidify again and almost laughed in excitement as it snapped back into place with a soft hum, Bilhaeder's connection as solid as it had ever been.

His own power now shut off from the plane's connection, Xeoniteridone lashed at me with sorcery, my own blocking him, swelling out beyond me and swooping toward him to take him down at last. I felt his pain and laughed as I tried to catch him again. *I hope I didn't hurt you too badly.*

He snarled at me, the image of him pale, favoring one side even as a gaping black hole formed beside him. *I should have killed you.*

The feeling is mutual, I sent. *Let's rectify that now, shall we?*

I almost had him. I could feel the fear in him as he realized just how strong my sorcery was, his shock and sudden need to escape. My power lunged for him even as he threw two of his people in my path, jerking their magic to intercept mine while he fled through the gaping hole he'd made in the veil and vanished.

I snapped back to myself as he left, sinking to Mabel's

warm back while she circled the city, Max on her wing.

Well done, Ahbi sent.

We almost had him, I sent, fury rising.

And next time, Mabel sent, *we will. Victory, no matter how it comes about, is still victory, Meira. You proved you can stop him—and the loss of Demonicon. I say that is a win.*

Me, too, Syd sent, waving from Max's back. *We'll go after him.*

I'm coming with you. I urged Mabel forward, but the drach ignored me.

You go home, Syd sent. *We won't catch him, he's too clever. But we can force him to run, at least, while you finish healing.*

Frustration fought a pitched battle with my need to finish what I started. But, as my sister and Max soared through a tear in the veil, I knew she was right. Next time I faced down Xeoniteridone, I would be ready for him.

He had just damned well hope he was ready for me.

I sat next to Ram once again, holding his hand while Portlish shook his head.

"Still not quite right," he muttered. "I'm sorry, Ruler. I'm close, but I'm missing something."

I just nodded, tired but unable to sleep knowing Ram was down here by himself. It turned out they were taking shifts, Zinnia and Pagomaris, watching him and keeping him from devouring the magic around him.

"You are right about many things," Portlish said, one

foot shifting, his crooked body bending over my love. "I think, without the nectar—a constant control over his sorcery—he is a danger to everyone, including himself."

"He would drain everything around him if we did not hold him back," Zinnia said. It was her turn, but she'd stepped back to allow me to sit with Ram.

"Ram is attempting to feed not only his addiction," Portlish said, "but his sorcery."

How well I understood that. "So Xeoniteridone is using the nectar to control them and their sorcery, making it possible for him to channel it." Confirmation was a good thing.

"Keeping them docile would be a benefit," Portlish said. "It's how I'd do it." He winced, lowered his head. "Apologies, Ruler. But I am a criminal."

I reached out to him and took his hand. "You are a valuable member of my team," I said. "And I expect full honesty."

The cook bobbed a nod, his thin neck seeming to struggle to hold up his big head. "Thank you, Ruler," he said.

"I'm more worried about what this means if they continue to grow in numbers," I said. "I was able to counter Xeoniteridone because he wasn't expecting me this time. But he knows what I can do, now. And he will be waiting for me."

At least no more of the Node had gone missing since

the attack on Bilhaeder.

"He has much to answer for," Zinnia said. "As does Henemordonin."

Ahbi grunted, but didn't comment and neither did I. We both had plans for my grandfather and I didn't care for anyone to know what they were until it was too late for him.

Far too late.

Looking down at Ram made me wince. The fact I'd trusted Elphremantic made things worse. How could I let him kiss me, while my darling Ram...?

Don't torture yourself, Ahbi sent. *Meira*.

"Ruler." Portlish gestured at Ram. "I hate to bear more bad news." His hands ran over the wisps of his hair, wobbling his big ears. "I must either find an antidote in the next few days or give him more nectar, which makes my job harder."

"Or?" I didn't need the answer. I already knew it from the look of Ram, how wasted he'd become.

"I'm afraid we'll lose him," Portlish said.

I waved him off and he bowed to me before hobbling his way out. My fingers traced down Ram's cheek, into the stubble on his cleft chin, over the faint scar of the cut I'd given him had left behind. I remembered his smile, his caring, the way he said my name. And did my best not to cry.

"We will save him," Zinnia said, fierce, voice full of

tears.

We would. No matter what, not matter the cost. I would never let him go.

CHAPTER TWENTY EIGHT

My throne was hard under me, the weight I'd lost to the nectar nightmare I'd endured most telling. Ahbi kindly built a cushion of power, shielding me from the worst of it, but I could still feel the chill seeping into my bones.

As I stared over the gathered court, I thought of my sister and wished I could join her. Be anywhere but here, glowering at the family who brought me so low. She'd come to see me before I convened this morning, with no real news.

"We tried to track him," she said, dropping into one of my chairs while Max stood quietly next to Mabel. "But he's slippery."

"Indeed," Max said as Sassafras hopped into Syd's arms for some scratches. "He certainly knows how to use his sorcery to the very utmost of its ability."

"Is that admiration I hear?" Mabel's lip twitched.

"Even the most vile of creatures manage the occasional brilliant quality," Max said.

"At least we now know you can beat him," Syd said over Sassy's purr. "That's huge."

I nodded, shaking hands clasped behind my back. She was confident enough for both of us, though I'd lost some of my detachment since gaining a troubled night's sleep filled with bad dreams. "I can," I said. "And it is."

"Time to declare war on his ass." Syd stood, setting Sass down on the cushion.

"At least put an end to the recruitment," Sassafras said.

Just that simple. "I'll do my best," I said. "Though I believe the fact he ran means he's done converting demons and has shifted focus to the Node." A quick visit the night before and a sorcerous shield around the shrinking collection of plane energy had blocked him for now.

"Anything you need," Syd said.

I glanced at the drach who both shifted slightly in tandem.

"You have your own job to do," I said. "Max?"

He nodded slowly. "We have been away from the battle with the veil's damage for too long," he said. "Forgive me, but I, at least, must go."

"I'm not leaving her," Mabel said in a voice gone

deep with what sounded like the beginning of an argument.

"No," Max said, the corners of his mouth lifting. "I don't imagine you are."

Syd waffled and Syd wavered but, in the end, Syd went with Max. Before they left, though, I had a thought.

"Could it be," I said, "what Xeoniteridone is up to is somehow feeding your issue?"

Max looked startled, an odd expression for a drach. "How so?"

Syd's eyes flew wide. "Oh. My. Swearword. Meems is right." She spun on the big drach. "He's tampering with the veil," she said. "Those ripples we've felt…"

Max nodded once, sharply, tearing open a gap beside him, already moving. "Of course," he said. "We must go. And Ruler," he paused, "thank you."

I felt a little better as the veil snapped shut behind them. Maybe I wasn't so confident in myself just yet, but at least I'd offered some help to save the veil.

Mabel watched me as I unclenched my hands and shook them out, trying to summon the strength to go to court.

"There is no shame in what you've experienced," she said. "The only shame would be giving in now, after so much has happened."

I smiled at her, small and fragile, but there. My insides felt fractured, my entire being trembling as I did my best to block out the rising tide of feelings threatening to take over. My weakness gone, it was replaced with a different kind of tired, a bone-weary, soul-deep exhaustion come from going to hell and back again.

Two deep breaths and I found the courage, my faithful Sassafras at my feet, and the drach following behind.

I'd encountered Bakari on the elevator, feeling him long before he appeared as he followed me to the lift.

"Don't kill Xeoniteridone," I said into the thin air just as the assassin's sorcery began to ripple and make him visible. "Or Henemordonin. Or Elphremantic. And, most especially, not Tanasharia."

Bakari frowned. "Accidents happen," he said.

I snapped at him with power, Ahbi snarling while my sorcery hit him in the chest and drove him to the edge of the elevator, the shields keeping him from falling.

"I want them all," I said, turning my back on him. "Don't forget it."

"Very well," Bakari said. "I will tell my order to capture, not kill."

I glanced sideways at him as he rejoined me, the elevator settling at the entrance to the throne room, but didn't move to leave the platform. "That was easy."

He shrugged. "You have proven you are the right demon for the job after all," he said. "And, in doing so, have won the faith of my leaders."

I shifted on my throne at the memory, my sorcery reaching out and touching the multitude of new minds surrounding me. The assassin's order now surrounded me with their numbers, hidden among the court as fresh eyes and ears. No one questioned their welcome, a small fact I embraced.

It was comforting to know they were there, and for the first time since I took First Seat, I wasn't under the constant pressure to fail and quit. Even the court bowed to me, their fear real, their need for me to save them so powerful I almost choked on it.

My sorcery stirred inside me, the monster craving their power. It would be easy to replace the lost magic of Demonicon—magic I could no longer use anyway, even if I did have access—through the black of my sorcery. I found myself embracing it more and more, felt it affecting my moods, pulling me more often to the dark. I knew without Ahbi there to keep me in balance, it would be simple to accept and embrace the black fully.

No, she sent to me as I shifted yet again in my seat. *You would never do such a thing. But I am happy to be here to help you.*

I wasn't so sure. My gaze drifted sideways, to the empty Second Seat while I let the court stir and wait for me to address them.

Just as long as Syd's trust—their trust, finally hard won—wasn't misplaced. It was difficult to accept I was allowing the monster inside me to have her way, the monster I feared and hated for so long.

Meira, Ahbi sent. *If you weren't worried, I would be. Now, let's end this.*

I straightened on my throne and felt her reach out with her power, embracing the entirety of the massed demons in the throne room, my sorcery humming and siphoning power from the Seat itself. It needed to feed, and where better to draw magic from? At least I didn't then have to feel guilty for taking energy from the demons before me, as much as they deserved it.

"From this moment," I said, knowing Ahbi pushed my voice forward and upward, echoing it back from the shielding above, "I declare martial law on all of Demonicon. We are now at war, not only with the Planeless and their leader, Xeoniteridone, but I also charge Henemordonin, former Second Seat and pretender to the First Seat an enemy of our people. He will, upon sight, be arrested and brought before us for punishment."

Even his most hard-core supporters didn't peep, bowing to me with hope on their pathetic faces.

"And last," I said, standing as a pool of blackness opened beneath me in counter point to Ahbi's magic, "I declare myself Ruler, that Second Seat will remain empty until that time I will fill it, and all control of Demonicon falls to me."

They could have argued. Henemordonin still

possessed the power of Demonicon. I was a pretender at this point, without the magic I needed to claim the throne. But it was clear from their attitude not one of them was willing to step up. And as far as I was concerned, I had simply taken back what they'd fought to steal from me, but more—I was demanding a true dictatorship, without a Second Seat to temper my judgments or the power of Demonicon to secure my rule.

"When this crisis is over," I said, my words met with acquiescent silence, "a new order shall be created, one that serves all demons. Until then, I take full responsibility for the safety and protection of our world. And I will not fail you."

They had the nerve to cheer while inside I quavered.

We'll be fine, Ahbi sent. *You'll see.*

I would, indeed.

Like what you read? Find out more at
pattilarsen.com

Here's a look at the first chapter of
Book Three of the First Plane Trilogy

RULER

chapter one

The hunched and twisted little demon bent over, one unmarred hand clasping a glass vial of pale purple liquid. Sloshing accompanied a counterpoint of low moaning rising from the emaciated demon half-conscious on the slab bed. I held myself very still in the chill air of the cell as Portlish, the nectar cook, tipped the vial over Rameranselot's lips and allowed the thick stream to pour, mist swirling from the mouth of the bottle, between his parched lips.

My thick, black fingernails dug into the palms of my hands in the effort it took not to lunge forward and knock the cook aside, to protect the demon I loved from more torture. Because it was torture, plain and simple. Every dose of the newest attempt at an antidote Portlish tried to create ended in the same result—agony for Ram and utter failure.

And yet, I couldn't bring myself to lose hope. As Ruler of my people, I had to believe there was a way to save not only Ram, but all of the demons lost to the Planeless cult. The new breed of nectar created by their leader, Xeoniteridone, was being used to suppress demon power in order to allow their sorcery to arise. The cult leader's rapid success stripped me of the vast majority of my guards as well as put Demonicon at risk of utter failure. The sorcery the cult leader had access to rapidly disassembled the Node holding my world together, breaking it into its component planes, rendering it back to its original, fractured state. And there was very little I could do about it.

Without an antidote to the nectar, without the means to bring my demon subjects back into control of their elemental magic—and their minds—Demonicon was, ultimately, doomed. Not even my sister, Syd, saver of worlds and powerful maji, had been able to put a stop to the degradation. And the mighty drach, first race born of the Creator, were also stumped, my friend and ally, Mabel, as ineffective as the rest of us.

Yes, I'd managed to keep Xeoniteridone from severing one of the planes during an actual confrontation. But tracking him down in order to do so again was proving almost impossible. I'd tried a few times in the last thirty-six hours, chasing ghosts and shadows as he dipped into Demonicon from wherever he hid and stole another plane from me before I could even muster myself to follow. He'd learned not to face me directly, that much was clear. It might have been comforting to know I could defeat him one-on-one, but I had to find him first. Which meant he seemed determined to ensure we never had such a confrontation again.

At least, not until he knew he could defeat me. And leaving the next time and place to his discretion made me incredibly nervous.

My teeth ached from clenching them, hands almost numb from balling my fists as I waited for the inevitable. My mind might wander during these times of testing, but my focus remained with the pale and sweating demon stretched out on the cold stone slab, his precious face turned away from me. When he didn't react immediately to the dose, Portlish leaned back with a hopeful half-smile.

An expression which shifted to disappointment and frustration as the first convulsions took over Ram's body.

I wrapped my power around him, sorcery all that was available to me, though my grandmother's spirit still had full control of her own demon power. Ahbi stayed back, out of my way. She'd tried a few times to assist, and only seemed to make things worse, her magic drawing howls of pain from Ram. Instead, I soothed him with the blackness of my hungry energy, drawing out the agony into the dark as he writhed and tears streamed from the corners of his eyes.

For one moment, they flickered open as Ram's head tossed to the side, his gaze meeting mine. I barely recognized him, his sunken cheeks, pink skin once burnished red and deep-set eyes seeming to sink into his skull. But when our gazes met, I saw a flash in him, the note of recognition, and I finally did let hope swell inside me.

"Ram," I whispered, holding my ground, trembling from the effort.

"Meira," he croaked. I saw his throat working, knew he fought the control the nectar had over him, tried to say more. My feet moved without my permission, knees bending, my hands cupping his cheeks. Points of moisture landed on his face as my tears finally took over, and I crumpled under the weight of what was happening to him.

"Ram," I said. "Fight it. Please."

He gargled something, one hand rising in a whip-like motion, thinned fingers digging into the flesh of my arm. And then his eyes rolled back in his head, body arching upward, a seizure sending powerful tremors through his body. No amount of sorcery could ease his suffering, though I tried. When he finally collapsed, I was sobbing, caring less Portlish saw, nor that Ram's aunt, Zinnia, once my father's fiancée, watched with her own terrible sadness on her face.

"I'm sorry, Ruler," Portlish said in his velvet voice. "I don't know what I'm missing." His own frustration came through loud and clear, though I couldn't bring myself to feel sympathy for him. Still, I managed to hold back the snapping response I longed to throw at him, demanding a solution.

It wasn't Portlish's fault. And anger would solve nothing at this point.

I rose from the edge of Ram's stone slab bed, stepping away as he passed into troubled unconsciousness. Zinnia's hand caught mine as I stepped away, holding me there. Her clear gaze held too much empathy, far too much. She would make me cry all over again.

"Progress," she said. "He's never spoken before."

I glanced at Portlish who shrugged. "Perhaps," he said with a deep sigh. "Perhaps."

Hope whimpered in my heart and curled into a ball of defeat.

"No more," I said, voice shaking despite everything I did to keep it level. "He can't take any further testing."

Zinnia didn't comment, stroking her nephew's damp forehead with her free hand. Portlish didn't argue, either, though his next statement was obvious.

"I must have a subject to test," he said, tone low and apologetic. "I'm sorry."

I nodded brusquely, turning from Ram, wiping at the

tears on my face, the offensive things. "The next dose," I said, "you test on me."

"Ruler." Zinnia's disapproval did nothing to change my mind. "We've had this conversation."

"We have," I snapped at last, refusing to look at her. "Although you may think your Daeva leader has a right to tell me what to do, I will remind you I am still Ruler." Even if my own advisors agreed with them. As far as I was concerned, the secretive and meddling Daeva had no say in my decisions. They'd spent the last few millennia making sure no Ruler knew what they were up to. Until me. And now only because they were finally in over their heads and needed my help. I wasn't in a charitable mood when it came to Zinnia's order and didn't know if I'd ever be again.

"I need my power back," I said, the waver gone from my voice. A tidy lie, but not completely dishonest. I had access to demon magic through my grandmother, but I needed access and control over my own. And yet, my present upset was about Ram, and we all knew it. While finding a cure for him meant also finding one for me and all the other demons lost to Xeoniteridone and the Planeless cult, I was less worried about my people than the suffering figure on the slab before me. He moaned in time with my thoughts as I stepped forward and jabbed Portlish in one crooked shoulder with my finger. "Find the cure," I said. "And bring it directly to me when you're done."

Portlish bowed to me, gaze flickering to Zinnia before settling on me again. "I'm doing my best, my Ruler," he said, distress in his entire twisted body. "I swear I am."

"I know." I softened, patting the same spot I'd just prodded. "But we're running out of time." I really didn't need to state the obvious. Everyone around me knew just how imminent the fall of Demonicon was, even Portlish, mostly locked in the lab that had been Theridialis's. Not for the first time, I thought with regret about the old demon scientist and his loss, purportedly to the Planeless. I knew, with his help, we would have had a cure by now—most likely the reason he'd been kidnapped in the first place.

But he wasn't here, and Portlish, formerly a nectar street cook, was all I had.

I shuddered as I felt a sliver of the Node leave, so in tune with it through my sorcery I was aware of every single loss the moment it happened. Ahbi shivered inside me in echo to my reaction, though she remained silent as she had been over the last day and a half. I found I missed my grandmother's constant flow of chatter and, despite the struggles we'd faced finding balance between the two of us, wished she would at least be one thing in my life that felt normal.

Avenesequoia, one of my closest advisors and the sister to my beloved silver Persian/demon boy, Sassafras, poked her head in the doorway, face composed though I knew her heart was breaking for Ram from her refusal to look at him.

"Ruler," she said in her light voice. "Jabuticabron has returned."

I nodded to her, pausing one last moment to bend and press my lips to Ram's feverish brow. He muttered something I didn't catch before sighing and falling into a deeper sleep. His heart rate slowed, almost dangerously so, and I knew I was right to stop the testing. As strong as he was, Ram wouldn't survive much more of this, and his loss I would never accept.

Squaring myself for the world above the cell where he was held, I settled my Ruler persona around me and followed Sequoia out into the hall, the fear I'd return to find Ram gone forever rising with familiar agony even as my feet carried me away from him.

about the author

Everything you need to know about me is in this one statement: I've wanted to be a writer since I was a little girl, and now I'm doing it. How cool is that, being able to follow your dream and make it reality? I've tried everything from university to college, graduating the second with a journalism diploma (I sucked at telling real stories), am part of an all-girl improv troupe (if you've never tried it, I highly recommend making things up as you go along as often as possible). I've even been in a Celtic girl band (some of our stuff is on YouTube!) and was an independent film maker. My life has been one creative thing after another—all leading me here, to writing books for a living.

Now with multiple series in happy publication, I live on beautiful and magical Prince Edward Island (I know you've heard of Anne of Green Gables) with my very patient husband and multitude of pets.

I love-love-love hearing from you! You can reach me (and I promise I'll message back) at patti@pattilarsen.com. And if you're eager for your next dose of Patti Larsen books (usually about one release a month) come join my mailing list! All the best up and coming, giveaways, contests and, of course, my observations on the world (aren't you just dying to know what I think about everything?) all in one place: http://smarturl.it/PattiLarsenEmail.

Last—but not least!—I hope you enjoyed what you read! Your happiness is my happiness. And I'd love to hear just what you thought. A review where you found this book would mean the world to me—reviews feed writers more than you will ever know. So, loved it (or not so much), **your honest review would make my day**. Thank you!